THE OWL SERVICE

Alan Garner was born in Cheshire on 17th October 1934, and his childhood was spent in Alderley Edge, where his family has lived for more than four hundred years. His attendance at the local primary school was interrupted by several serious illnesses, from three of which he nearly died.

At the age of eleven he went to Manchester Grammar School, and became the fastest schoolboy sprinter in Britain.

Before going to Oxford, he spent two years' National Service as a lieutenant in The Royal Artillery. Realising then that his original ambition to become Professor of Greek was no longer valid, he decided to become a writer. He found his present mediaeval house, dug himself in, and wrote.

Since then, he has produced fifteen books, a film adaptation, two television adaptations, three television plays and an original film script. Amongst his awards are The Lewis Carroll Shelf Award, The Phoenix Award of America, and the First Prize at the Chicago International Film Festival for writing and presenting his film *Images*.

Of himself, he says: "I am essentially lazy, and have no interest in stirring myself to be mediocre."

Collins Modern Classics

The Owl Service

by

Alan Garner

illustrated by
Bob Harvey

Collins
An imprint of HarperCollinsPublishers

The author acknowledges with thanks the use of the following copyright material:
The Bread of Truth by R. S. Thomas (Rupert Hart-Davis);
The Mabinogion: translated by Gwyn Jones and Thomas Jones
(J. M. Dent & Sons); The Radio Times, The British Broadcasting Corporation.

First published in Great Britain by William Collins Sons & Co. Ltd 1967
First published as a Collins Modern Classic 1998

5 7 9 10 8 6 4

Collins Modern Classics is an imprint of
HarperCollins*Publishers* Ltd, 77-85 Fulham Palace Road,
Hammersmith, London W6 8JB

The HarperCollins website address is
www.fireandwater.com

ISBN 0 00 675401-5

Printed and bound in Great Britain by
Omnia Books Limited, Glasgow

For Cinna

—The owls are restless.
People have died here,
Good men for bad reasons,
Better forgotten.—
    R. S. Thomas

I will build my love a tower
By the clear crystal fountain,
And on it I will build
All the flowers of the mountain.
    Traditional

Possessive parents rarely live long enough
to see the fruits of their selfishness.
    Radio Times (15.9.65)

Contents

NOTE: I am indebted to Betty Greaves, who saw the pattern; to Professor Gwyn Jones and Professor Thomas Jones, for permission to use copyright material in the text; and to Dafydd Rees Cilwern, for his patience.

A.G.

CHAPTER ONE

"How's the bellyache, then?"

Gwyn stuck his head round the door. Alison sat in the iron bed with brass knobs. Porcelain columns showed the Infant Bacchus and there was a lump of slate under one leg because the floor dipped.

"A bore," said Alison. "And I'm too hot."

"Tough," said Gwyn. "I couldn't find any books, so I've brought one I had from school. I'm supposed to be reading it for Literature, but you're welcome: it looks deadly."

"Thanks anyway," said Alison.

"Roger's gone for a swim. You wanting company are you?"

"Don't put yourself out for me," said Alison.

"Right," said Gwyn. "Cheerio."

He rode sideways down the banisters on his arms to the

first floor landing.

"Gwyn!"

"Yes? What's the matter? You OK?"

"Quick!"

"You want a basin? You going to throw up, are you?"

"Gwyn!"

He ran back. Alison was kneeling on the bed.

"Listen," she said. "Can you hear that?"

"That what?"

"That noise in the ceiling. Listen."

The house was quiet. Mostyn Lewis-Jones was calling after the sheep on the mountain: and something was scratching in the ceiling above the bed.

"Mice," said Gwyn.

"Too loud," said Alison.

"Rats, then."

"No. Listen. It's something hard."

"They want their claws trimming."

"It's not rats," said Alison.

"It is rats. They're on the wood: that's why they're so loud."

"I heard it the first night I came," said Alison, "and every night since: a few minutes after I'm in bed."

"That's rats," said Gwyn. "As bold as you please."

"No," said Alison. "It's something trying to get out. The scratching's a bit louder each night. And today — it's the loudest yet — and it's not there all the time."

"They must be tired by now," said Gwyn.

Chapter One

"Today – it's been scratching when the pain's bad. Isn't that strange?"

"You're strange," said Gwyn. He stood on the bed, and rapped the ceiling. "You up there! Buzz off!"

The bed jangled as he fell, and landed hard, and sat gaping at Alison. His knocks had been answered.

"Gwyn! Do it again!"

Gwyn stood up.

Knock, knock.

Scratch, scratch.

Knock.

Scratch.

Knock knock knock.

Scratch scratch scratch.

Knock – knock knock.

Scratch – scratch scratch.

Gwyn whistled. "Hey," he said. "These rats should be up the Grammar at Aberystwyth." He jumped off the bed. "Now where've I seen it? – I know: in the closet here."

Gwyn opened a door by the bedroom chimney. It was a narrow space like a cupboard, and there was a hatch in the ceiling.

"We need a ladder," said Gwyn.

"Can't you reach if you stand on the washbasin?" said Alison.

"Too chancy. We need a pair of steps and a hammer. The bolt's rusted in. I'll go and fetch them from the stables."

"Don't be long," said Alison. "I'm all jittery."

" 'Gwyn's Educated Rats': how's that? We'll make a packet on the telly."

He came back with the stepladder, hammer and a cage trap.

"My Mam's in the kitchen, so I couldn't get bait."

"I've some chocolate," said Alison. "It's fruit and nut: will that do?"

"Fine," said Gwyn. "Give it us here now."

He had no room to strike hard with the hammer, and rust and old paint dropped in his face.

"It's painted right over," he said. "No one's been up for years. Ah. That's it."

The bolt broke from its rust. Gwyn climbed down for Alison's torch. He wiped his face on his sleeve, and winked at her.

"That's shut their racket, anyway."

As he said this the scratching began on the door over his head, louder than before.

"You don't have to open it," said Alison.

"And say goodbye to fame and fortune?"

"Don't laugh about it. You don't have to do it for me. Gwyn, be careful. It sounds so sharp: strong and sharp."

"Who's laughing, girlie?" He brought a dry mop from the landing and placed the head against the door in the ceiling. The scratching had stopped. He pushed hard, and the door banged open. Dust sank in a cloud.

"It's light," said Gwyn. "There's a pane of glass let in the roof."

Chapter One

"Do be careful," said Alison.

"'Is there anybody there?' said the Traveller' – Yarawarawarawarawara!" Gwyn brandished the mop through the hole. "Nothing, see."

He climbed until his head was above the level of the joists. Alison went to the foot of the ladder.

"A lot of muck and straw. Coming?"

"No," said Alison. "I'd get hayfever in that dust. I'm allergic."

"There's a smell," said Gwyn: "a kind of scent: I can't quite – yes: it's meadowsweet. Funny, that. It must be blowing from the river. The slates feel red hot."

"Can you see what was making the noise?" said Alison.

Gwyn braced his hands on either side of the hatch and drew his legs up.

"It's only a place for the water tanks, and that," he said. "No proper floor. Wait a minute, though!"

"Where are you going? Be careful." Alison heard Gwyn move across the ceiling.

In the darkest corner of the loft a plank lay over the joists, and on it was a whole dinner service: squat towers of plates, a mound of dishes, and all covered with grime, straw, droppings and blackened pieces of birds' nests.

"What is it?" said Alison. She had come up the ladder and was holding a handkerchief to her nose.

"Plates. Masses of them."

"Are they broken?"

"Nothing wrong with them as far as I can see, except

muck. They're rather nice – green and gold shining through the straw."

"Bring one down, and we'll wash it."

Alison saw Gwyn lift a plate from the top of the nearest pile, and then he lurched, and nearly put his foot through the ceiling between the joists.

"Gwyn! Is that you?"

"Whoops!"

"Please come down."

"Right. Just a second. It's so blooming hot up here it made me go sken-eyed."

He came to the hatch and gave Alison the plate.

"I think your mother's calling you," said Alison.

Gwyn climbed down and went to the top of the stairs.

"What you want, Mam?"

"Fetch me two lettuce from the kitchen garden!" His mother's voice echoed from below. "And be sharp now!"

"I'm busy!"

"You are not!"

Gwyn pulled a face. "You clean the plate," he said to Alison. "I'll be right back." Before he went downstairs Gwyn put the cage trap into the loft and closed the hatch.

"What did you do that for? You didn't see anything, did you?" said Alison.

"No," said Gwyn. "But there's droppings. I still want to know what kind of rats it is can count."

CHAPTER TWO

ROGER SPLASHED THROUGH the shallows to the bank. A slab of rock stood out of the ground close by him, and he sprawled backwards into the foam of meadowsweet that grew thickly round its base. He gathered the stems in his arms and pulled the milky heads down over his face to shield him from the sun.

Through the flowers he could see a jet trail moving across the sky, but the only sounds were the river and a farmer calling sheep somewhere up the valley.

The mountains were gentle in the heat. The ridge above the house, crowned with a grove of fir trees, looked black against the summer light. He breathed the cool sweet air of the flowers. He felt the sun drag deep in his limbs.

Something flew by him, a blink of dark on the leaves. It was heavy, and fast, and struck hard. He felt the vibration through the rock, and he heard a scream.

Roger was on his feet, crouching, hands wide, but the meadow was empty, and the scream was gone: he caught its echo in the farmer's distant voice and a curlew away on the mountain. There was no one in sight: his heart raced, and he was cold in the heat of the sun. He looked at his hands. The meadowsweet had cut him, lining his palm with red beads. The flowers stank of goat.

He leant against the rock. The mountains hung over him, ready to fill the valley. "Brrr—" He rubbed his arms and legs with his fists. The skin was rough with gooseflesh. He looked up and down the river, at the water sliding like oil under the trees and breaking on the stones. "Now what the heck was that? Acoustics? Trick acoustics? And those hills – they'd addle anyone's brains." He pressed his back against the rock. "Don't you move. I'm watching you. That's better – Hello?"

There was a hole in the rock. It was round and smooth, and it went right through from one side to the other. He felt it with his hand before he saw. Has it been drilled on purpose, or is it a freak? he thought. Waste of time if it isn't natural: crafty precision job, though. "Gosh, what a fluke!" He had lined himself up with the hole to see if it was straight, and he was looking at the ridge of fir trees above the house. The hole framed the trees exactly… "Brrrr, put some clothes on."

Roger walked up through the garden from the river. Huw Halfbacon was raking the gravel on the drive in front of the house, and talking to Gwyn, who was banging lettuces together to shake the earth from the roots.

"Lovely day for a swim," said Huw.

"Yes," said Roger. "Perfect."

"Lovely."

"Yes."

"You were swimming?" said Huw.

"That's why I'm wearing trunks," said Roger.

"It is a lovely day for that," said Huw. "Swimming."

"Yes."

"In the water," said Huw.

"I've got to get changed," said Roger.

"I'll come with you," said Gwyn. "I want to have a talk."

"That man's gaga," said Roger when they were out of hearing. "He's so far gone he's coming back."

They sat on the terrace. It was shaded by its own steepness, and below them the river shone through the trees. "Hurry up then," said Roger. "I'm cold."

"Something happened just now," said Gwyn. "There was scratching in the loft over Alison's bedroom."

"Mice," said Roger.

"That's what I said. But when I knocked to scare them away – they knocked back."

"Get off!"

"They did. So I went up to have a look. There's a pile of dirty plates up there: must be worth pounds."

"Oh? That's interesting. Have you brought them down?"

"One. Alison's cleaning it. But what about the scratching?"

"Could be anything. These plates, though: what are they like? Why were they up there?"

"I couldn't see much. I asked Huw about them."

"Well?"

"He said, 'Mind how you are looking at her.'"

"Who? Ali? What's she got to do with it?"

"Not Alison. I don't know who he meant. When I told him I'd found the plates he stopped raking for a moment and said that: 'Mind how you are looking at her.' Then you came."

"I tell you, the man's off his head. – Why's he called Halfbacon, anyway?"

"It's the Welsh: Huw Hannerhob," said Gwyn. "Huw Halfbacon: Huw the Flitch: he's called both."

"It suits him."

"It's a nickname," said Gwyn.

"What's his real name?"

"I don't think he knows. Roger? There's one more thing. I don't want you to laugh."

"OK."

"Well, when I picked up the top plate, I came over all queer. A sort of tingling in my hands, and everything went muzzy – you know how at the pictures it sometimes goes out of focus on the screen and then comes back? It was like that: only when I could see straight again, it was different somehow. Something had changed."

"Like when you're watching a person who's asleep, and they wake up," said Roger. "They don't move, nothing happens, but you know they're awake."

"That's it!" said Gwyn. "That's it! Exactly! Better than what I was trying to say! By, you're a quick one, aren't you?"

"Can you tell me anything about a rock with a hole through it down by the river?" said Roger.

"A big slab?" said Gwyn.

"Yes, just in the meadow."

"It'll be the Stone of Gronw, but I don't know why. Ask Huw. He's worked at the house all his life."

"No thanks. He'd give me the London Stockmarket Closing Report."

"What do you want to know for, anyway?" said Gwyn.

"I was sunbathing there," said Roger. "Are you coming to see how Ali's managed with your plate?"

"In a sec," said Gwyn. "I got to drop these in the kitchen for Mam. I'll see you there."

Roger changed quickly and went up to Alison. His bedroom was immediately below hers, on the first floor.

She was bending over a plate which she had balanced on her knees. The plate was covered with a sheet of paper and she was drawing something with a pencil.

"What's this Gwyn says you've found?" said Roger.

"I've nearly finished," said Alison. She kept moving the paper as she drew. "There! What do you think of that?" She was flushed.

Roger took the plate and turned it over. "No maker's mark," he said. "Pity. I thought it might have been a real find. It's ordinary stuff: thick: not worth much."

"Thick yourself! Look at the pattern!"

"Yes. – Well?"

"Don't you see what it is?"

"An abstract design in green round the edge, touched up with a bit of rough gilding."

"Roger! You're being stupid on purpose! Look at that part. It's an owl's head."

"—Yes? I suppose it is, if you want it to be. Three leafy heads with this kind of abstract flowery business in between each one. Yes: I suppose so."

"It's not abstract," said Alison. "That's the body. If you take the design off the plate and fit it together it makes a complete owl. See. I've traced the two parts of the design, and all you do is turn the head right round till it's the other way up, and then join it to the top of the main pattern where it follows the rim of the plate. There you are. It's an owl – head, wings and all."

"So it's an owl," said Roger. "An owl that's been sat on."

"You wait," said Alison, and she began to cut round the design with a pair of scissors. When she had finished she pressed the head forward, bent and tucked in the splayed legs, curled the feet and perched the owl on the edge of her candlestick.

Roger laughed. "Yes! It is! An owl!"

It was an owl: a stylised, floral owl. The bending of its legs had curved the back, giving the body the rigid set of an owl. It glared from under heavy brows.

"No, that's really good," said Roger. "How did you think

it all out – the tracing, and how to fold it?"

"I saw it as soon as I'd washed the plate," said Alison. "It was obvious."

"It was?" said Roger. "I'd never have thought of it. I like him."

"Her," said Alison.

"You can tell? OK. Her. I like her." He tapped the owl's head with the pencil, making the body rock on its perch. "Hello there!"

"Don't do that," said Alison.

"What?"

"Don't touch her."

"Are you all right?"

"Give me the pencil. I must make some more," said Alison.

"I put the lettuce by the sink," Gwyn called. "I'm going to see Alison."

"You wait, boy," said his mother. "Them lettuce need washing. I only got one pair of hands."

Gwyn slashed the roots into the pig bucket and ran water in the sink. His mother came through from the larder. She was gathering herself to make bread. Gwyn tore the leaves off the lettuce and flounced them into the water. Neither of them spoke for a long time.

"I told you be sharp with them lettuce," said his mother. "You been back to Aber for them?"

"I was talking," said Gwyn.

"Oh?"

"To Roger."

"You was talking to Halfbacon," said his mother. "I got eyes."

"Well?"

"I told you have nothing to do with him, didn't I?"

"I only stopped for a second."

"You keep away from that old fool, you hear me? I'm telling you, boy!"

"He's not all that old," said Gwyn.

"Don't come that with me," said his mother. "You want a back hander? You can have it."

"There's slugs in this lettuce," said Gwyn.

"You was speaking Welsh, too."

"Huw doesn't manage English very clever. He can't say what he means."

"You know I won't have you speaking Welsh. I've not struggled all these years in Aber to have you talk like a labourer. I could have stayed in the valley if I'd wanted that."

"But Mam, I got to practise! It's exams next year."

"If I'd known you was going to be filled with that squit you'd never have gone the Grammar."

"Yes, Mam. You keep saying."

"What was you talking about, then?"

"I was only asking Huw if he could tell me why those plates were in the roof above Alison's room."

The silence made Gwyn look round. His mother was leaning against the baking board, one hand pressed to her thin side.

"You not been up in that roof, boy."

"Yes. Alison was − a bit bothered, so I went up, and found these plates. I didn't touch − only one. She's cleaning it."

"That Alison!" said Gwyn's mother, and made for the stairs, scraping her floury arms down her apron. Gwyn followed.

They heard Alison and Roger laughing. Gwyn's mother knocked at the bedroom door, and went in.

Alison and Roger were playing with three flimsy cut out paper models of birds. One was on the candlestick and the other two were side by side on a chair back. The plate Gwyn had brought from the loft was next to Alison's pillows and covered with scraps of paper. Alison pushed the plate behind her when Gwyn's mother came in.

"Now, Miss Alison, what's this about plates?"

"Plates, Nancy?"

"If you please."

"What plates, Nancy?"

"You know what I mean, Miss Alison. Them plates from the loft."

"What about them?"

"Where are they?"

"There's only one, Mam," said Gwyn.

"Gwyn!" said Alison.

"I'll trouble you to give me that plate, Miss."

"Why?"

"You had no right to go up there."

"I didn't go."

"Nor to send my boy up, neither."

"I didn't send him."

"Excuse me," said Roger. "I've things to do." He ducked out of the room.

"I'll thank you not to waste my time, Miss Alison. Please to give me that plate."

"Nancy, you're hissing like an old goose."

"Please to give me that plate, Miss Alison."

"Whose house is this, anyway?" said Alison.

Gwyn's mother drew herself up. She went over to the bed and held out her hand. "If you please. I seen where you put it under your pillow."

Alison sat stiffly in the bed. Gwyn thought that she was going to order his mother from the room. But she reached behind her and pulled out the plate, and threw it on the bed. Gwyn's mother took it. It was a plain white plate, without decoration.

"Very well, Miss Alison. Ve-ry well!"

Nancy went from the room with the plate in her hand. Gwyn stood at the door and gave a silent whistle.

"You ever played Find the Lady, have you?" he said. "'Now you see it, now you don't.' Who taught you that one, girlie?"

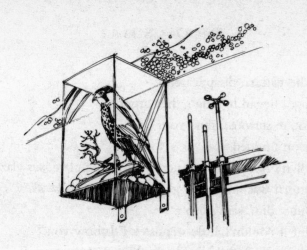

CHAPTER THREE

"You've caused a right barny," said Roger. "Nancy's been throwing her apron over her head and threatening I don't know what, your mother's had a fit of the vapours, and now Nancy's on her dignity. She's given my Dad her notice three times already."

"Why doesn't he accept it?" said Alison.

"You should know Dad by now," said Roger. "Anything for a quiet life: that's why he never gets one. But you'd a nerve, working that switch on her. Pity she knew the plates were decorated. How did you manage it?"

"I didn't," said Alison.

"Come off it."

"I didn't. That was the plate I traced the owls from."

"But Gwyn says you gave Nancy an ordinary white one."

"The pattern disappeared."

Roger began to laugh, then stopped.

"You're serious, aren't you?"

Alison nodded.

"Ali, it's not possible," said Roger. "The plate was glazed: the pattern was under the glaze. It couldn't rub off."

"But it did," said Alison.

"But it couldn't, little stepsister. I'll show you."

Roger climbed the ladder and opened the trap door.

"It's too dark. Where's your torch?"

"Here," said Alison. "Can you see the plates? They're in a corner over to your left."

"Yes. I'll bring a couple to prove they're all the same."

"Bring more. As many as you can. Let's have them. Hand them down to me."

"Better not," said Roger: "after the tizz. But I don't think these'll be missed."

"Mind the joists," said Alison. "Gwyn nearly fell through the ceiling there. It was queer."

"I bet it was!"

"No. Really queer. He slipped when he touched the plate, and he went all shadowy. Just for a second it didn't look like Gwyn."

"It's the darkest part of the loft," said Roger.

They washed the plates and took them to the window. Roger scrubbed the glaze with a nailbrush. "The glaze is shot," he said. He picked at it with his fingernail. "It comes off easily."

"All right," said Alison. "I want to trace these owls before the light goes. I'm making them properly this time, out of stiff paper."

"Not more!" said Roger. "Why do you want more? Where are the three you did earlier?"

"I couldn't find them."

"If you're going to start that drawing again, I'm off," said Roger. "When you've done one you've done them all. Shall I take your supper things down?"

"I've not had supper," said Alison.

"Hasn't Dad been up with your tray?"

"No."

Roger grinned. "Your mother sent him to do the stern father act."

"He's not come."

"Good old Dad," said Roger.

Roger went downstairs and out through the kitchen to the back of the house. He listened at the door of a long building that had once been the dairy but was now a billiard-room. He heard the click of ivory.

Roger opened the door. His father was playing snooker by himself in the dusk. A supper tray was on an armchair.

"Hello, Dad," said Roger.

"Jolly good," said his father.

"I'll light the lamps for you."

"No need. I'm only pottering."

Roger sat on the edge of the chair. His father moved round the table, trundling the balls into the pockets, under the eyes of the falcons and buzzards, otters, foxes, badgers and pine martens that stared from their glass cases on the wall.

"Don't they put you off your game?" said Roger.

"Ha ha; yes."

"This room was the dairy, wasn't it?"

"Oooh, yes, I dare say."

"Gwyn was telling me. He thinks it might have been the original house before that – an open hall, with everybody living together."

"Really?" said his father. "Fancy that."

"It often happens, Gwyn says. The original house becomes an outbuilding."

"Damn," said Roger's father. "I'm snookered." He straightened up and chalked his cue. "Yes: rum old place, this."

"It's that olde worlde wall panelling that gets me," said Roger. "I mean, why cover something genuine with that phoney stuff?"

"I thought it was rather tasteful, myself," said his father.

"All right," said Roger. "But why go and pebble-dash a piece of the wall? Pebble-dash! Inside!" A rectangle of wall near the door was encrusted with mortar.

"I've seen worse than that," said his father. "When I started in business I was on the road for a few years, and there was one Bed-and-Breakfast in Kendal that was grey pebble-dashed all over inside. Fifteen-watt bulbs, too, I remember, in every room. We called it Wookey Hole."

"But at least it was all over," said Roger. "Why just this piece of wall?"

"Damp?"

"The walls are a yard thick."

"Still," said his father, "it must be some weakness somewhere. It's cracked."

"Is it? It wasn't this morning."

"Right across, near the top."

"That definitely wasn't there this morning," said Roger. "I was teaching Gwyn billiards. We tried to work out what the pebble-dash was for. I looked very closely. It wasn't cracked."

"Ah, well it is now," said his father. "Not much use doing any more tonight. Let's pack up."

They collected the balls, stacked the cues and rolled the dustsheet over the table.

"Would you like me to take Ali her supper?" said Roger.

"Yes – er: no: no: I said I would: I'd better. Margaret thinks I ought. She's a bit upset by the fuss."

"How's Nancy?"

"Phew! That was a real up-and-downer while it lasted! But I think we've managed. A fiver cures most things. She's dead set against some plates or other – I didn't understand what any of it was about. No: I'd better go and chat up old Ali."

Alison was cutting out the last owl when she heard her stepfather bringing the supper tray. She had arranged the plates on the mantelpiece and had perched the owls about the room as she finished them. He pushed the door open with his shoulder and came in backwards.

"Grub up!"

"Thanks, Clive," said Alison. "What is it?"

"Nancy's Best Limp Salad, with sheep-dip mayonnaise." He put the tray by the bed and lit the lamp. "I say, these are jolly fellows. What are they?"

"Owls. I made them."

"They're rather fun."

"Yes."

"Well – er: how are the gripes?"

"Much better, thanks."

"Good. Up and about this morning?"

"What sort of a day did you and Mummy have?" said Alison.

"Didn't catch anything, and one of the waders leaked, but I've great hopes of tomorrow. Old Halfwhatsit says he knows a stretch of the river where they always bite."

"I bet he didn't say where it is."

"Er – no. No, he didn't."

"Have you been sent to tell me off about Nancy?"

"What? Oh. Ha ha," said Clive.

"I don't know why she was going on like that," said Alison, "and I didn't see it had anything to do with her. Gwyn found some of those plates in the loft, and she came storming up as if she owned the place."

"Yes. Well. Old Nance, eh? You know—"

"But she went berserk, Clive!"

Chapter Three

"Too true. We had a basinful when we came home, I'll tell you! Your mother's very upset. She says you ought to — oh well, skip it."

"But it's my house, isn't it?" said Alison.

"Ah yes."

"Well then."

"It's a bit dodgy. If your father hadn't turned it over to you before he died your mother would've had to sell this house to clear the death duties. Morbid, but there it is."

"But it's still my house," said Alison. "And I don't have to take orders from my cook."

"Fairs do's," said Clive. "Think of your mother. It was hard enough to get someone to live in all summer. If Nance swept out we'd never find a replacement, and your mother would have to cope by herself. She'd be very upset. And it is the first time we've all been together — as a family, and — and — you know?"

"Yes, Clive. I suppose so."

"That's my girl. Now eat your supper. — Hello: sounds as if we've mice in the roof."

"Don't wait, Clive," said Alison. "I'm not hungry. I'll eat this later, and bring the tray down in the morning. Tell Mummy not to worry."

"That's my girl. God bless."

CHAPTER FOUR

"AND THE ROOM was so cold," said Roger. "It was like being in a deepfreeze. But it was the noise that was worst. I thought the ceiling was coming in. And there were scratchings going on round her bed, too, on the wall and then on the iron and her supper tray – you could tell the difference. Is that what you heard when you went up the loft?"

"No, not as bad," said Gwyn. "But she said it was getting louder. What did you do, man?"

"I called her, but she was fast asleep."

"What time was it?"

"About one o'clock," said Roger. "You know how hot it was last night – I couldn't sleep, and I kept hearing this noise. I thought she was having a nightmare, and then I thought perhaps she was ill, so I went up."

"The noise was in the loft? You're sure?"

"Positive. It was something sharpening its claws on the joists, or trying to get out, and either way it wasn't funny."

"You're absolutely certain it couldn't have been rats?"

"I don't know what it was," said Roger, "but it sounded big."

"How big?"

"Big enough."

"Then what?"

"Nothing – I funked out," said Roger. "I couldn't stand it."

"How is she this morning?"

"She was all right at breakfast, a bit queasy, but that's all."

"Where is she now?"

"She said she was going to find her paper owls. She's obsessed with those futile birds."

"Them off the plates?" said Gwyn.

"Yes. Do you know how they got into the loft?"

"My Mam won't say anything about them – nothing that sticks together: she's that mad. And the switch Alison put across her! By! It's making her talk like a Welsh Nationalist!"

"Ali says she didn't switch the plate."

"Pull the other," said Gwyn. "It's got bells on."

"That's what I said to her yesterday. But she didn't switch."

"Ring-a-ding-a-ding," said Gwyn.

"Listen. I fetched two more down from the loft, and

when I went into Ali's bedroom last night they were on the mantelpiece. The pattern's gone."

"How did you know?" said Alison. She stood at the door of the billiard-room with the plates in her hand. "I was coming to show you."

"Er — I thought I heard you having a bad dream last night," said Roger, "so I popped in. The plates were on the mantelpiece."

"Yes: they're the same, aren't they?" said Gwyn. "Well now, there's a thing."

"How can it happen?" said Alison. "Is it tracing the owls that makes the plates go blank?"

"What did you use?" said Roger. "Pumice?"

"Let's see the owls." said Gwyn.

"I haven't any."

"What?" said Roger. "You've done nothing else but make owls."

"They keep disappearing."

"This is ridiculous," said Gwyn.

"Has your mother said anything?" said Alison.

"Not that can be repeated: except she's made it a condition of staying that the loft's nailed up permanent."

"Today?"

"Now there she's hoist by her own petard, like. It's stupid. She won't let Huw Halfbacon in the house."

"What does she have against him?" said Alison.

"Search me," said Gwyn. "Anyway, I measure the hatch, then Huw makes a cover, and I nail it up. We can spin that out till tomorrow between us. Plenty of time to bring the plates down, isn't it?"

"How about leaving them where they are?" said Roger.

"We can't," said Alison. "I must make some owls."

Roger shrugged.

"We'll have to be a bit crafty," said Gwyn. "Mam's propped the kitchen door open. She'd hear us easy if we tried to carry them down."

"That woman!" cried Alison. "She's impossible!"

"I know what you mean, Miss Alison," said Gwyn.

There was a scream from the kitchen.

"That's Mam!" said Gwyn, and they looked out of the billiard-room. Nancy appeared at the outside door of the larder with a broken plate in her hands.

"Oh!" she shouted. "Oh! Throwing plates now, are you? That's it! That's it! That's it, Miss! That's it!"

"What's the matter?" said Alison.

"Don't come that with me, Miss! I know better! So sweet and innocent you are! I know! Spite and malice it is!"

"What's the matter?" shouted Roger.

"I know my place," said Nancy. "And she should know hers. I was not engaged to be thrown at! To be made mock of – and dangerous too! Spite, Miss Alison! I'm not stopping here!"

"It was me," said Gwyn. "I was fooling about. I didn't see the door was open, and I didn't see you there. The plate slipped. Sorry, Mam."

Nancy said nothing, but stepped back and slammed the

door. Gwyn beckoned the other two away.

"Wow," said Roger. "What was that?"

"Thanks, Gwyn," said Alison. Gwyn looked at her. "I couldn't help it," she said.

"Couldn't you?"

"Will somebody tell me what's going on round here?" said Roger.

"Forget it," said Gwyn. "I'd better go and butter up the old darling. Don't worry, I can handle her all right. I'm going down the shop this morning, so I'll buy her a packet of fags to keep her happy."

"She looked wild," said Alison.

"Do you blame her?" said Gwyn. "And what's a clip on the earhole among friends? You go and square your family, put them wise, get in first: just in case. I'll calm Mam down, and then we'll see to the loft. She's touchy this morning because I'm not supposed to speak to Huw, and I must over this job."

"But what happened then?" said Roger. "That plate was the one she took from Ali's room yesterday, wasn't it?"

"I know," said Gwyn. "Where are the others?"

"I·put them on the billiard table," said Alison.

"I'll pick them up on my way back," said Gwyn. "We'll have a good look at them later."

"Who's going to deal with which?" Alison said to Roger as they walked across the lawn.

"We'll each tackle our own, I think, in this case," said Roger.

Chapter Four

"Mummy's sunbathing on the terrace," said Alison.

"Right. Dad's in the river somewhere, I expect, trying out his puncture repairs. Peculiar business, isn't it? You know just before Nancy yelled — when you were letting off steam about her — a crack went right through that pebble-dash in the billiard-room. I saw it. It was behind you. Peculiar that. It's the second since yesterday. Dad spotted one last night."

Gwyn walked slowly. The plate had been on the dresser in the kitchen: his mother had been in the larder: a difficult shot. Who could have done it? Huw was shovelling coke by the stables. Who would have done it?

The smash in the billiard-room was like an explosion. Gwyn ran. The fragments of the plates lay on the floor. They had hit the wall where it was pebble-dashed, and the whole width of the mortar near the top was laced with cracks. Gwyn looked under the table and in the cupboards, but no one was hiding, and the animals were motionless in their glass.

Very gently, and softly, trying to make no noise, Gwyn gathered up the pieces. The morning sun came through the skylights and warmed the oak beams of the roof. They gave off a sweet smell, the essence of their years, wood and corn and milk and all the uses of the room. A motorcycle went by along the road above the house, making the glass rattle.

Gwyn heard something drop behind him, and he turned. A lump of pebble-dash had come off the wall, and another fell, and in their place on the wall two eyes were watching him.

CHAPTER FIVE

"GWYN SAID HE'D done it. I don't think she believed him, but she had to shut up."

"Good," said Clive. "His head's screwed on."

"Yes, Gwyn's all right," said Roger. "But I thought you'd better know, in case Nancy wants to make a row over it."

"Too true," said Clive.

"None of us chucked the plate," said Roger.

"It probably fell, and the old girl thought someone had buzzed her," said Clive. "That seems to have fixed my puncture." He lumbered out of the river. "Dry as a bone."

"Have you seen this, Dad?" said Roger. He was sitting on top of the upright slab. "This hole?"

"Oh? No."

"Any ideas how it was made?" said Roger. "It goes right through."

"So it does. Machine tooled, I'd say. Lovely job. Seems a rum thing to do out here in the wilds."

"Have a squint from the other side, up towards the house."

Roger's father put his hands on his knees and bent to look through the hole.

"Well I never," he said. "Fancy that."

"It frames the top of the ridge, and the trees, doesn't it?"

"Like a snapshot."

"That's a point," said Roger. "I wonder if it's possible. You'd need a heck of a focal depth, and the camera I've brought here only stops down to f.16. It'd be interesting, technically – You're off shopping today, aren't you?"

"Yes: back after tea, I expect. That's the drag of this place. It's a day's job every week."

"I'll need a different film and paper," said Roger. "Can you buy it for me?"

"Surely. But write it down, old lad."

Gwyn locked the billiard-room door, and instead of putting the key back on its hook in the kitchen he kept it in his pocket and went down the narrow path between the back of the house and the high retaining wall of the steep garden. He moved in a green light of ferns and damp moss, and the air smelt cool.

When he reached the open lawn he sat on the edge of the fish tank and rinsed his hands. Grey lime dust drifted from his fingers like a cobweb over the water. He bit a torn nail smooth, and cleaned out the sand with a twig. Then he went to the stables.

At first he thought that Huw must have finished with the coke, but when he came to the yard he saw Huw leaning on his shovel, and something about him made Gwyn stop.

Huw stood with two fingers lodged in his waistcoat pocket, his head cocked sideways, and although his body seemed to strain he did not move. He was talking to himself, but Gwyn could not hear what he said, and he was dazzled by the glare of the sun when he tried to find what Huw was looking at. Then he saw. It was the whole sky.

There were no clouds, and the sky was drained white towards the sun. The air throbbed, flashed like blue lightning, sometimes dark, sometimes pale, and the pulse of the throbbing grew, and now the shades followed one another so quickly that Gwyn could see no more than a trembling which became a play of light on the sheen of a wing, but when he looked about him he felt that the trees and the rocks had never held such depth, and the line of the mountain made his heart shake.

"There's daft," said Gwyn.

He went up to Huw Halfbacon. Huw had not moved, and now Gwyn could hear what he was saying. It was almost a chant.

"Come, apple-sweet murmurer; come, harp of my gladness; come, summer, come."

"Huw."

Chapter Five

"Come, apple-sweet murmurer; come, harp of my gladness; come, summer, come."

"Huw?"

"Come, apple-sweet murmurer; come, harp of my gladness; come, summer, come."

Huw looked at Gwyn, and looked through him. "She's coming," he said. "She won't be long now."

"Mam says you're to make a board to nail over the loft in the house," said Gwyn. "If I measure up, can you let the job last till tomorrow?"

Huw sighed, and began to shovel coke. "You want a board to nail up the loft, is that what you said?"

"Yes, but we need time to bring the plates down without Mam finding out."

"Be careful."

"Don't you worry."

"I'll do that for you," said Huw.

"Why has Mam taken against you?"

"You'd better ask her. I've no quarrel."

"She's been away from the valley all these years. You'd think she'd have got over any old rows. But she hasn't spoken to you, has she?"

"Perhaps she is afraid in the English way," said Huw. "But if they think I am weak in the head they should have seen my uncle. And grandfather they would lock in their brick walls."

"Why?"

"Grandfather?" said Huw. "He went mad, down through the wood by the river."

"Here?" said Gwyn. "The wood in the garden, where it's swampy?"

"Yes. We don't go there."

"Really, really mad?" said Gwyn.

"That's what the English said. They would not let him stay here. He lost his job."

"The English? Wasn't the house lived in properly even then?"

"It has never been a home," said Huw. "They come for a while, and go. And my grandfather had to go. They would not let him stay in the valley."

"What happened to him?"

"He walked away. Sometimes we heard of him. He sent those plates. He was working in the big potteries, and he decorated the plates and sent them to the house, and a letter to say he was all right now, but word came soon after that he had died at Stoke."

"But why were they put in the loft? And why did Mam have hysterics when I found them?"

"Ask her. She's your mother," said Huw. "Perhaps there's always talk in a valley."

"Is there anything needed for the house while we're out shopping, Halfbacon?"

Roger and his father came into the yard.

"No, sir," said Huw. "We are not wanting any stuff."

"Good," said Clive. "I'll be off, then. Jot down what you want for your snaps, won't you, Roger? Funny rock you have in the meadow, Halfbacon. Who drilled the hole in it?"

"It is the Stone of Gronw," said Huw.

"Oh? What's that when it's at home, eh? Ha ha."

"There is a man being killed at that place," said Huw: "old time."

"Was there now!"

"Yes," said Huw. "He has been taking the other man's wife."

"That's a bit off, I must say," said Clive. "I suppose the stone's a kind of memorial, eh? But who made the hole? You can see those trees through it at the top of the ridge."

"Yes, sir," said Huw. "He is standing on the bank of the river, see, and the husband is up there on the Bryn with a spear: and he is putting the stone between himself and the spear, and the spear is going right through the stone and him."

"Oho," said Clive.

"Why did he stand there and let it happen?" said Roger.

"Because he killed the husband the same way earlier to take the wife."

"Tit for tat," said Clive. "These old yarns, eh? Well, I must be off."

"Yes, sir, that is how it is happening, old time."

Gwyn went with Roger and his father towards the house.

"Will you be using the billiard-room today, Mr Bradley?"

"No," said Clive. "I'll be fishing as soon as we're back: mustn't waste this weather, you know. Help yourself, old son."

"Here's what I want for my camera, Dad," said Roger. "It's all there."

"Fine," said Clive. "Well, cheerio."

"I was beginning to believe that maundering old liar," said Roger.

"Huw wasn't lying. Not deliberate," said Gwyn.

"What? A spear making that hole? Thrown all the way from those trees? By a stiff?"

"Huw believes it."

"You Welsh are all the same," said Roger. "Scratch one and they all bleed."

"What happened to you yesterday by the Stone of Gronw?" said Gwyn. "You knew what I meant when I was trying to explain how it felt when I picked up a plate. And then you started talking about the stone out of nowhere."

"It was a feeling," said Roger. "One minute everything's OK – and the next minute it's not. Too much clean living, I expect. I'll cut down on the yoghurt—"

"And you came straight up from the river," said Gwyn. "Didn't you? Work it out, man. We both felt something, and it must have been near enough at the same time. What was it?"

"A thump," said Roger. "A kind of scream. Very quick. Perhaps there was an accident—"

"I've not heard of any," said Gwyn. "And in this valley you can't sneeze without everyone knowing from here to Aber."

"There was a whistling, too," said Roger, "in the air.

That's all."

"And I got a shock from the plates," said Gwyn. "And nothing's been the same since. Did you notice the sky when you were with your Dad a few minutes ago?"

"No?"

"Flashing," said Gwyn. "Like strip lighting switched on, only blue."

"No," said Roger.

"Huw saw it. Where's Alison?"

"Gone to tell her mother about yours."

"There's something to show you," said Gwyn. "In the billiard-room."

They found Alison rattling the door handle. "Why have you locked it?" she said. "I want the plates."

"They're still here," said Gwyn.

He unlocked the door and they went inside.

"Gwyn! You've broken them!"

"Not me, lady. Have you seen what's behind you?"

"Holy cow!" said Roger.

CHAPTER SIX

SHE WAS TALL. Her long hair fell to her waist, framing in gold her pale and lovely face. Her eyes were blue. She wore a loose gown of white cambric, embroidered with living green stems of broom and meadowsweet, and a wreath of green oak leaves in her hair.

"Gave me quite a turn, she did," said Gwyn. "There was just her eyes showing at first, but that pebble-dash soon came off."

"She's so beautiful!" said Alison. "Who'd want to cover her up?"

"Sixteenth century, if it's a day," said Roger. "Fresh as new. How's it survived under that lot?"

The woman was painted life-size in oils on wooden panelling. She stood against a background of clover heads spaced in rows.

Chapter Six

"What a find!" said Roger. "It'll fetch thousands."

"Not so fast," said Gwyn. "We'll keep our mouths shut. You'll have to organise your Dad, and the one person who mustn't know is my Mam."

"Why, for heaven's sake? Don't you realize? You've a masterpiece here."

"My Mam would take an axe to it," said Gwyn. "Start thinking. You've not asked me how I found it."

"How did you, then?" said Alison.

"It was your plates. I was coming back in here when I heard them smash. They'd been chucked against the pebble-dash, and a piece fell off."

"Why should this make your mother wreck it?" said Alison.

"My Mam's scared stiff about something. She's grim at the best of times, but not this bad. It's the plates, isn't it, Alison?"

"How should I know?"

"Guessing; and what Huw said. 'Mind how you are looking at her,' and now in the yard, 'She's coming,' he said."

"What does that mean?" said Roger.

"You can't tell. He could be talking about the weather. It's called 'she' in Welsh."

"Then that's it," said Roger.

"But if it isn't?" said Gwyn. "Someone cared enough about the painting and the plates to lug a dinner service into the roof and to pebble-dash this wall. You don't go to all that trouble for nothing. Somebody wanted them hidden, and now they're not hidden. They're – loose."

"It might not have been the same person. And there's no harm, whatever the reason is," said Alison, "not if we find something as wonderful as this."

"Have you looked close? Marvellous detail, isn't it?" said Gwyn.

"Every strand of hair," said Roger. "I can't get over how it's stayed so clean all this time."

"Marvellous," said Gwyn. "Have you looked at them clover heads, boyo?"

"Great stuff: like heraldry," said Roger. He went right up to the panelling. "And yet you could pick them—" Roger stepped back. "Oh no," he said.

"What's the matter?" said Alison. She looked. The heads were formed of curved white petals bunched together, each painted separately, fine and sharp. But the petals were not petals: they were claws.

"Someone had a nasty mind," said Roger.

"Or maybe that's the way it was when they painted it," said Gwyn. "Nasty."

"You can't have flowers made of claws," said Roger.

"Why not? You can have owls made of flowers, can't you?" said Gwyn. "Let's bring the plates down. I want to see them close to – and with the pattern on. Leave this pebble-dash: I'll clear it up later. And don't say anything about this wall until we've had a think."

They arranged that Gwyn and Roger should take the plates out of the loft and lower them from the bedroom window in a linen basket to Alison, who would be waiting with a barrow.

"I'm getting cold feet over this," said Roger. "Shouldn't we leave it as it is, and nail the loft up?"

"There's something in this valley," said Gwyn, "and my Mam's on to it. She's been like the kiss of death since she saw them plates. That clover: them plates: it's owls and flowers, and it's dangerous."

"So nail the loft up," said Roger. "If you'd seen Ali last night you wouldn't be keen."

"That's why I'm shifting the plates," said Gwyn. "Get them away from her first, and then we can think. I've not had a proper look at them paper models she makes: are they genuine?"

"Absolutely. I've watched her. It's dead clever the way she traces the patterns out so it fits together."

"Does she really keep losing them?"

"I think so," said Roger. "She's quite het up about it."

"So I've noticed," said Gwyn. "We must disconnect her."

"Disconnect?"

"That's about it. Batteries can't work without wires."

Gwyn went up into the loft, and handed the dinner service to Roger, who put it in the linen basket and lowered it on a rope to Alison, then Gwyn measured the hatch, and came down.

"You know, I think we're being a bit overwrought about all this," said Roger. "When you see them they are just plates. And perhaps it was just mice."

"Mice," said Gwyn. "I'd forgotten. I set a cage trap."

He climbed up the ladder and opened the hatch. Roger could see him from the waist down. He stood very still.

"Have you caught anything?" said Roger.

"You've seen a cage trap, haven't you?" said Gwyn. "You know how it works – a one-way door: what's in it can't get out: right?"

"Yes," said Roger. "Have you caught anything?"

"I think I've caught a mouse," said Gwyn.

" 'Think'?"

Gwyn came down the ladder. He held out the cage. Inside was a hard-packed ball of bones and fur.

"I think it's a mouse," he said. "Owls aren't fussy. They just swallow straight off, and what they don't want they cough up later. That's an owl's pellet: but I think it was mouse."

CHAPTER SEVEN

THEY HAD NOT heard Nancy come up the stairs. She was in the bedroom doorway.

"It's taking you long enough to measure that door, isn't it, boy?" she said. "Is that all you're doing? What you need that trap for?"

"I've finished, Mam," said Gwyn. "I'm going down the shop."

"About time," said Nancy. "I'm wanting flour for tea scones: be sharp."

"Can I have my money now?" said Gwyn.

"You has pocket money Saturday," said Nancy.

"I know, Mam. Can I have it early this week?"

"You think I'm made of it? There's nothing as can't wait. Saturday, boy."

"But Mam—"

"Down the shop with you, and less cheek."

"I'm not cheeking you."

"You are now," said Nancy.

Gwyn went downstairs and into the kitchen. Roger followed. Gwyn opened a cupboard and took his mother's purse from behind a cocoa tin.

"You're not going to nick it, are you?" said Roger.

"No," said Gwyn.

"You don't need cash for the flour," said Roger. "It goes on the account."

"Yes," said Gwyn.

"Do you have pocket money every week?" said Roger.

"Yes."

"Bit quaint, isn't it?"

"Is it?"

"Though if that's how you're fixed I suppose it's OK to take some early. You're not pinching it — just anticipating."

"Not even that," said Gwyn. "I'm giving." He opened the purse, and dropped the ball of mouse inside. "A poor thing, but mine own." Then he closed the purse, and put it back in the cupboard.

Gwyn walked so fast down the drive that Roger had to run after him. His face was white and he did not speak.

"Should you have done that? It might give her heart failure," said Roger. "After all, she is your mother."

"After all," said Gwyn, "she is."

"What did you want your money for?"

"Ten lousy fags."

Chapter Seven

"Oh."

"Ten stinking fags."

"Look," said Roger. "If that's all it is, I can lend you—"

"No thanks."

"You needn't give it me back. I get plenty."

"Congratulations."

"What's up with you?"

"Nothing."

"Look. Stick it on the account at the shop. It'll never be noticed."

"No thanks."

"You make me puke," said Roger.

The shop was in the front room of a cottage half a mile down the valley. The room was furnished to be lived in. There was a table of black oak, carved with herons, and on top an empty red plastic tomato that had once held sauce but was now an ornament. Jars of boiled sweets were on the sideboard among wedding photographs, and beside a grandfather clock were two dustbins holding sugar and flour. The ceiling was so low that a hole had been dug in the floor for the clock to stand in. Mrs Richards, the shopkeeper, was talking to Mrs Lewis-Jones in Welsh.

"I've been expecting it, Mrs Lewis-Jones, I've been expecting it. There was never a summer like it this week, and then Gareth Pugh's black sow ran wild on the mountain and they can't bring her down. Grandad used to say the beasts always know first."

"They do," said Mrs Lewis-Jones. "They're very excitable,

like a baby on with its teeth. We can't come near our old bull, and the sheep are right up on the top there. Mr Lewis-Jones is out all hours mending fences as far as the Ravenstone."

"That's a long way!" said Mrs Richards.

"I'll have two thin-sliced," said Mrs Lewis-Jones.

"We've no bread yet," said Mrs Richards. "The postman hasn't been."

"To think we shall see it in our time, Mrs Richards!"

"Is it certain?"

"It is. Mister Huw came to tell us last night. He was going to all the farms. He says she is coming, and it's owls."

"The poor things!" said Mrs Richards, and she looked sideways at Roger and Gwyn.

"Could we have—" said Roger.

"One minute, if you please," said Mrs Richards. She cut a lump of butter from a block on the windowsill. "Is it to be the three of them again, Mrs Lewis-Jones?"

"Yes. There's the girl, too. Mister Huw says she's made it owls."

"We must bear it," said Mrs Richards. "There's no escaping, is there? Aberystwyth isn't far enough."

"You've said a true word there, Mrs Richards. "I'll have a packet of soap flakes."

"Excuse me," said Roger. "If you've a lot of shopping, I wonder if we could possibly have some flour. We're in rather a hurry."

"Certainly," said Mrs Lewis-Jones. "Are you the young gentleman from up the house?"

"Yes," said Roger.

"There's nice," said Mrs Lewis-Jones. "And you Nancy's Gwyn, are you?"

"I'm Gwyn."

"There's nice. I was girl with your Mam. You having a nice time?"

"Yes – thanks," said Roger.

"Good," said Mrs Lewis-Jones. "It is a nice valley for the holiday."

"Six pound of flour for the house, please, Mrs Richards," said Gwyn.

"Righto, boy." Mrs Richards dipped a scoop into one of the dustbins. "She's coming, then?"

"She's coming," said Mrs Lewis-Jones. "The poor lady."

"If it takes that long to ask for half a pound of rancid butter and a packet of Daz I'm glad I don't speak Welsh," said Roger when they were outside. "I thought we were going to be there all day."

"They were talking," said Gwyn.

"And how," said Roger. "What about, anyway?"

"The weather."

"Typical," said Roger. "Women. Hey, I didn't see old Ali when we came out, did you?"

"No."

"I hope she managed those plates without being nabbed. Queer do about the trap, wasn't it? I wonder what made her put that grisly mouse in. I'd have thought she was too squeamish, even for a laugh."

"No laugh," said Gwyn. "And she didn't."

"She must have."

"She didn't. It was still warm."

"You're joking," said Roger. "I'd like to see the owl that could take a mouse out of a trap, eat it, and spit the pips back in."

"I shouldn't," said Gwyn.

"You know, it's darned rude of them, speaking Welsh like that," said Roger. "How would they have liked it if we'd started up in French?"

"Very thoughtless, yes: seeing as they're Welsh round here."

"Keep your shirt on," said Roger. "You were behind me: you didn't hear: they were speaking English until we went in."

"What were they saying?"

"Something about some bigwig coming. I didn't catch it. They clicked into Welsh when they saw me. Some kind of centenary, is it? A festival? A May Queen, or something? I don't know."

They walked under the shadow of the Bryn and along the drive. Alison was sitting in a deck chair on the lawn reading a book.

"Hi, Ali," said Roger. "Did you manage to stash the plates OK?"

Alison's eyes were hidden behind the black discs of her sunglasses.

"What plates?" she said.

CHAPTER EIGHT

"Aw, PLAY THE other side, Ali," said Roger.

"What are you talking about?"

"Hah," said Roger. "Hah. Hah. Hah. Is that better?"

"Yes thank you, Roger," said Alison, and went back to her book.

"Where's them plates?" said Gwyn.

"What plates?" said Alison, without looking from the page.

"Don't come that."

"I don't make a practice of 'coming' anything. Now may I read my book, please?"

"Where've you put them plates, you stupid nit?"

"Please," said Alison. "You're not at home now."

"Don't come that with me, girl!"

"And don't talk to me like that. You'll be sorry."

"And who'll make me? You, you jumped-up snob? You and who else? We got to have them plates! They're loaded!"

"Give him a lollipop, will you, Roger?" said Alison. "He's just like his mother."

Gwyn lashed out with his foot and kicked the book from Alison's hands, It landed yards away, splayed on the grass.

No one moved. There was silence. Then, "You shouldn't have done that," Alison said.

"You shouldn't have done that." Her knuckles were white on the edge of the deck chair. Her neck was thrust forward. "You shouldn't have done that."

Gwyn could see himself reflected in her sunglasses, and at the corner of the lens something fluttered like a wounded bird. He turned his head. It was the book. It came for him through the air. Its pages rattled, and disintegrated, but still came for him, like a tail after the red binding. Gwyn dropped the flour bags and protected his face as the book swarmed at him.

"No!" he shouted.

Gravel from the drive stung his hands and ears.

"Stop!"

Gwyn ran.

A heap of grass clippings exploded on his back, moist and sour, and pine cones showered his head. He blundered across to the wood, and the chippings fell away, but now twigs and leaves and pebbles and dead branches from the trees spun at him. A flour bag burst, and the next hit him, but he ran down towards the river, until there were only the living branches whipping him as he forced himself through. A few spent pebbles smacked in the mud by the boundary fence where Gwyn hung, sobbing, against the wire.

He looked past his shoulder, but no one had followed, and there was nothing except the wood. On the other side of the fence were the river and the mountain. He was over his shoes in the marsh.

The wood lay still. The air throbbed with insects, and flies hovered and disappeared and hovered. Meadowsweet grew in a mist of flowers, and the sun glinted on the threads of caterpillars which hung from the trees as thick as rain.

"By," said Gwyn, "there's axiomatic."

He thrust himself off the fence and walked uphill out of the marsh. He stopped at the two splashes of flour. From here there was a trail of litter towards the house. He rubbed his head, and some paper stuck to his hand, fragments of the book. Not only had the leaves disintegrated, but the paper itself was in shreds. He tried to read one of the scraps: it made no sense, but he recognized the print.

"Dicky Nignog!" cried Gwyn. "Dicky flaming Nignog!" He snatched another piece off the ground. It was the same print, from the same book. "Dicky Nignog," he groaned. But then a word caught his eye, and Gwyn looked closely. He read:

> – and enchantment to conjure a wife for him out of flowers',
> and he then a man in stature, and the handsomest youth that

mortal ever saw. And then they took the flowers of the oak, and the flowers of the broom, and the flowers of the meadowsweet, and from those they called forth the very fairest and best endowed maiden that mortal ever saw –

"Land of My Crumbling Fathers!" said Gwyn. He gathered more fragments, but he could do nothing with them. He followed the trail back through the wood, collecting the pieces, and at last he fitted two together.

– go in the form of a bird. And because of the dishonour thou hast done to Lleu Llaw Gyffes thou art never – thee wherever they may find thee; and that thou shalt not lose thy name, but that thou be for ever called Blodeuwedd."

Blodeuwedd is "owl" in the language of this present day. And for that reason birds are hostile to the owl. And the owl is still called blodeuwedd. –

"Dicky Nignog," said Gwyn. "Dicky, Dicky Nignog."

When Gwyn reached the house Alison and Roger were tidying the lawn.

"Have you the binding off that book?" said Gwyn.

"It's by the deck chair," said Alison.

Gwyn opened the cover. "Dicky Nignog," he said.

"Who?"

Gwyn pointed to the bookplate gummed inside the cover: Ex Libris R. St J. Williams. Llangynog. "Dicky Nignog," said Gwyn. "Our English master at Aber. He puts these labels everywhere. He's a raving book fetishist: washes his hands before reading. It nearly killed him to lend me this, but he said I had to read it, and the library copies were all out. He'll blow his top."

"I'm sorry," said Alison.

"Couldn't be helped," said Gwyn. "Looks like a wedding, doesn't it? Confetti by courtesy of R. St J. Williams, Esquire, B.A."

"Oh, Gwyn, I'm sorry."

"What was it like? You read it, did you?"

"Bits. They were short stories. Fine if you like that sort of thing – wizards and blood all over the place."

"Don't knock our National Heritage, girlie. Them old tales is all we got."

"What's the name of that stone again," Roger called, "down by the river?"

"The Stone of Gronw," said Gwyn.

"Is this the same?" said Roger. He was holding another scrap of paper.

– to Lleu, "Lord," said he, "since it was through a woman's wiles I did to thee that which I did, I beg thee in God's name, a stone I see on the river bank, let me set that between me and the blow." "Faith," said Lleu, "I will not refuse thee that." "Why," said he, "God repay thee." And then Gronw took the stone and set it between him and the blow. And then Lleu took aim at him with the spear, and it pierced through the stone and through him too, so that his back was broken, –

★ ★ ★

"I read that," said Alison.

"The whole story?" said Gwyn.

"I think so."

"Here, look at these. Is it all the same story?"

Alison read the other pieces.

"Yes: that's it."

"What's it about? What happened?" said Gwyn.

"Wait a minute," said Alison. "There was this wizard, or something, I forget his name, and he made a woman out of flowers, and she married this Clue Claw Somebody."

"Lleu Llaw Gyffes," said Gwyn.

"Yes: well then she fell in love with a man called Gronw: Gronw Pebyr. And he decided to kill Clue."

"Lleu."

"Clue."

"Never mind," said Gwyn. "Go on."

"This is a complicated bit: all magic," said Alison. "But Gronw threw a spear from a hill when Clue was standing by a river and killed him. But Clue wasn't really dead. He turned into an eagle, and the wizard found him and turned him back again. The wizard was his father, or uncle: I'm not sure. Then Clue and Gronw changed places, Clue threw the spear this time, and Gronw was killed. That's the end of the story."

"There's a stone by the river here called the Stone of Gronw," said Gwyn. "There's a hole in it."

"Which means we're right where all this Ku Klux Klan

is supposed to have happened, as Professor Halfbacon claims," said Roger. "Very interesting."

"Them plates," said Gwyn. "What happened to the wife?"

"Oh yes," said Alison. "The wizard said he wouldn't kill her; he'd do worse than that. So he turned her into an owl."

"I know what she said then," said Roger.

"What?"

" 'I haven't a Clue – hoo – hoo'!"

"Man," said Gwyn, "you're as daft as a clockwork orange."

CHAPTER NINE

"IT'S THE BEST I could manage," said Clive. "The chemist said he only stocked the normal tourist stuff, and he didn't have any of the developing gear. He said this film was very popular."

"Yes," said Roger. "It's the same as the one in my camera now. Never mind. It'll do. Thanks, Dad."

"Sorry if it's a washout," said Clive.

"No, it should be OK. These fast films don't enlarge as well as the one I wanted. They're a bit grainy, that's all."

"Are they, now?" said Clive.

"I'll go down to the river while there's light."

"I might see you," said Clive. "Should be able to put in an hour. Margaret's having a rest. By the way, is old Ali around?"

"Probably," said Roger. "I've not seen her since before

tea. Shall I give her a call?"

"Not to worry," said Clive. "It'll do later. I bought her a token of my esteem while we were out."

Clive took a small box from his pocket, and opened it. Inside were limpet shells of different sizes glued together, painted, and varnished, to make an owl.

"Got it from a place called Keltikrafts," he said. "Thought it might amuse her – she was cutting out some of these fellows last night, you know, and as soon as I saw it I thought, that's just the thing for old Ali. Look, there's some of the lingo on the back: 'Greetings from the Land of Song', it says. The young woman in the shop translated it for me. Will she like it?"

"She's mad for owls, anyway," said Roger.

He collected his tripod, camera and exposure meter, and went along the front drive. The drive curved past the stable yard and a gate in the wall led to the back of the stables, a dank place under the trees, where Huw Halfbacon chopped firewood. Garden rubbish was burnt here, next to an iron shed that was held up by the debris it was meant to protect. It was Huw's timber store: anything left from maintenance jobs was added to it, and over the years it had become a mess of fungus and corrugated rust, but this was not stopping Gwyn from trying to work himself towards the back of the pile.

Roger leant on the gate. "Having fun?" he said.

"She's put them somewhere," said Gwyn. "She's hidden them."

"But is that a likely place?" said Roger.

"I've tried the likely places," said Gwyn. "All of them: roof to cellar − greenhouses, stables, the lot. So that leaves the unlikely places, doesn't it?"

Roger climbed over to join Gwyn. "There's a whole dinner service, and that takes up space. You can see this dump's not been touched. Have you tried above the stables?"

There were three rooms over the stables, and because the stables were set into the hill the backs of these upper rooms had entrances at ground level. One of the rooms was used for table-tennis, and Roger had never been in the other two.

"I've looked in the big room," said Gwyn. "Huw lives next door and he has the only key, and the other's padlocked: none of the house keys fit − I've tried."

"They ought to," said Roger. "Let's see."

It was a heavy brass Yale lock, and no key fitted.

"You'll not shift that," said Gwyn.

Roger put his ear to the door. He beckoned to Gwyn. They both listened.

"There's someone moving about inside," Roger whispered. "Ali?" he called. "Ali?"

"Is that you, Alison?" said Gwyn.

There was no answer.

"What did you hear?" said Roger.

"Swishing," said Gwyn. "No footsteps."

"How would she get in?"

Chapter Nine

"There may be a connecting door from Huw's place. But that's locked."

"Ali," Roger called. "Ali. Don't muck about."

"Perhaps there's a way up from the stable," said Gwyn.

They went to look but found nothing, although they still heard the soft movement over their heads.

"I'm going to try the window," said Roger. "Give us a hand with this ladder."

They reared the ladder against the wall in the yard, and Roger climbed up while Gwyn stood on the bottom rung.

"I can't see much," said Roger. "The glass is all cobwebs inside. There's the door opposite – and something square, not very big, a crate, I think: and something black in a corner, but I can't see. It's an old junk room, that's all – nobody inside."

"It could be dead leaves in a draught," said Gwyn. "There's plenty by the door."

"Where've you tried?" said Roger when they put the ladder back in the stable.

"I said – all over the house, inside and out: even the kennels, and they're full of chicken wire."

"I'm going to use up my film by that stone," said Roger. "Coming?"

"What about Alison?"

"She's bound to be back for dinner in half an hour," said Roger. "And if she's not around the house we may find her by the river."

"But you don't realize," said Gwyn.

"I do," said Roger. "I was being dim on purpose. She couldn't have stood much more this afternoon, didn't you see? She was dead pale."

"What do you think it is?" said Gwyn.

"I don't know," said Roger. "I do know I wasn't imagining the row in her bedroom last night. The other business, when I thought I heard that shout – it could have been too much heat, I suppose. But last night was enough for me. If you'd seen it you'd have run."

"And this afternoon?" said Gwyn. "On the lawn?"

"Freak squall?" said Roger.

"Oh, man—"

"All right."

"And the plates going blank?"

"The glaze—"

"And smashing? And the billiard-room? And the pellet in the trap? And the owls? And flowers? And *The Mabinogion*?"

"The whation?" said Roger.

"That book," said Gwyn. "It's called *The Mabinogion*: 'the clear-running spring of Celtic genius', Dicky Nignog says. I used to think it was a load of old rope."

"Didn't mean much to me," said Roger. "What is it? Welsh myths?"

"Sort of," said Gwyn. "I wish I'd taken more notice."

"This is the stone," said Roger, "and the hole goes right through it."

"And the meadowsweet grew all around–around–

around," said Gwyn, "and the meadowsweet grew all around. You say the hole frames the trees on the Bryn? By, it does, too!"

"How is it you knew what the stone was if you've not seen it before?" said Roger.

"I know every cow-clap in this valley," said Gwyn. "I know where to look for sheep after a snowstorm. I know who built the bridge to Foothill Farm. I know why Mrs May won't go in the post office. I know how to find the slates that point the road over the mountain if you're caught in a mist. I know where the foxes go when they're hunted. I even know what Mrs Harvey knows! – And I came here for the first time last week! Makes you laugh, doesn't it? My Mam hates the place, but she can't get rid of it, see? It feels like every night of my life's been spent listening to Mam in that back street in Aber, her going on and on about the valley. She started in the kitchen here when she was twelve. There was a full staff in them days, not just Huw trying to keep the weeds down."

"Where's everybody gone to?" said Roger. "Most of the houses in the valley look empty."

"Who's going to rent to us when stuffed shirts from Birmingham pay eight quid a week so they can swank about their cottage in Wales?"

"Would you want to live here?"

"I ought to be in Parliament," said Gwyn.

He sat on the stone. "You're right," he said. "It's a long way for a spear. But you heard it, didn't you? And then he screamed."

"I don't count that. I'm only going on what I heard last night," said Roger.

"And the lawn this afternoon."

"You think it's haunted, then?"

"Ghosts don't eat mice," said Gwyn. "Whatever chewed that mouse could chew me or you."

"I give up," said Roger. "But if there's any more of it I'm off, I'll tell you."

"How will you manage?" said Gwyn.

"Dad's steerable when you know how."

"And the new Mrs Bradley?" said Gwyn. "A kind of family honeymoon, is it?"

"Mind your own business," said Roger. He spiked the tripod into the earth and set up the camera.

"What happened to your real Mam?" said Gwyn.

"I told you to mind your own business."

"She around then?"

Roger looked over the camera at Gwyn. "I'll fill you in," he said. "If you open your big mouth once more I'll fill you in."

"OK," said Gwyn.

"Right."

Gwyn concentrated on scratching his initials in the stone, and Roger bent to read the exposure meter, adjusted the lens.

"Not haunted," said Gwyn after a while. "More like – still happening?"

"A tenth at f.16," said Roger. "I'll go up and down either side of that: can't afford to change the stop, though. What did you say?"

"Gwydion. One of the Three Golden Shoemakers of the Isle of Britain. That's him."

"What are you blathering at?" said Roger.

"He was the wizard who made the wife out of flowers for Lleu Llaw Gyffes. It's coming back to me. We had it read at school a couple of years ago. Gwydion made Blodeuwedd for Lleu, and she fell in love with Gronw Pebyr—"

"That's what Alison said."

"And Gronw killed Lleu here on this very spot: then Lleu killed Gronw, and Blodeuwedd was turned into an owl—"

"The problem is to line the camera up with this hole, so that you can see the trees," said Roger, "but you have to be at least seven feet away, or you can't have the stone and the trees both in focus together. I want to use the rock texture as a frame for the trees in the distance. It should make an interesting composition."

"Think of it, man!" said Gwyn. "A woman made of flowers and then changed into an owl. The plates, man! It's all there if we could see it!" He jumped down and ran towards the house.

"Where are you off to?" shouted Roger.

"Huw the Flitch! 'Mind how you are looking at her.' He knows! The flamer!"

Roger went back to his camera. The light was fading quickly, and he decided to take the last frames of film on long exposures. He used the delayed setting for these. When he pressed the button the camera whirred for several seconds and then the shutter clicked. Whirr and click. Whirr and click. And the shadows seemed to come out of the river.

"Taking photos, are you?"

Roger yelped with fright. Huw Halfbacon was standing behind him. He was carrying some branches on his shoulder, and Roger had not heard him come along the river bank.

"What do you think you're doing, creeping up on me like that? I could have bust my camera!"

"I was bringing sticks," said Huw. "For the fire. Yes."

"Then why don't you fetch them from the wood?" said Roger. "It's choked with dead timber."

"We don't go there," said Huw.

"Why not?"

"Private."

"Private? Don't be stupid: that notice is to keep hikers out, not you."

"It is private family why we don't go in the wood," said Huw. "That is all." He swung his load to the ground and went down on one knee beside it. "You taking photo of the Stone of Gronw, are you?"

"No," said Roger. "The Albert Memorial."

"There's clever," said Huw.

Chapter Nine

Whirr. click.

"Do you mind?" said Roger. "I'm trying to finish this before dark. Gwyn's looking for you."

Huw began to suck at an unlit pipe, turning the charred bowl.

"It is old stone," he said. "The Stone of Gronw."

"I said, Gwyn's looking for you—"

"Not a bad man," said Huw. "He is not all to blame. She is setting her cap at him, the other man's wife."

"The one who was supposed to be made of flowers?" said Roger.

"Yes?" said Huw. "Blodeuwedd? You know her? You have raven's knowledge? Yes, she is setting her cap at him, the fine gentleman: Gronw Pebyr, Lord of Penllyn."

"Don't you people round here talk about anything else?" said Roger. "You'd think it was the only thing that's ever happened in this valley."

Whirr.

"That is right," said Huw.

Click.

"Finished," said Roger.

"Lleu is a hard lord," said Huw. "He is killing Gronw without anger, without love, without mercy. He is hurt too much by the woman and the spear. Yet what is there left when it is done? His pride. No wife: no friend."

Roger stared at Huw, "You're not so green as you're grass-looking, are you?" he said. "Now you mention it, I have been thinking. – That bloke Gronw was the only one with any real guts: at the end."

"But none of them is all to blame," said Huw. "It is only together they are destroying each other."

"That Blod-woman was pretty poor," said Roger, "however you look at it."

"No," said Huw. "She was made for her lord. Nobody is asking her if she wants him. It is bitter twisting to be shut up with a person you are not liking very much. I think she is often longing for the time when she was flowers on the mountain, and it is making her cruel, as the rose is growing thorns."

"Boy, you're really screwed up about this, aren't you?" said Roger. "And you'd have me as bad. I've been here a week and I've got the ab-dabs already. There's a world outside this valley, you know. It's not cherubs blowing their gaskets and a whale in the top left-hand corner."

"I been outside the valley," said Huw. "Once. That's why I'm Huw the Flitch."

"I don't see the connection," said Roger. He telescoped the tripod and slung the camera round his neck. "I must go," he said. "I'll be late for dinner."

"I am coming up the house," said Huw. "So I can tell you."

"All right," said Roger. "I'll buy it. Why are you called Halfbacon?"

"We are very short of meat in the valley, old time," said Huw. "And there is a man in the next valley. He has some pigs. But he is not letting anyone have them."

"So what did you do?"

"I go to him and I ask him to let me take the pigs in exchange for what I will give him."

"Fair enough," said Roger. "Did he agree?"

"Yes."

"And you took the pigs, and that's how you got your nickname."

"Yes." Huw laughed. "I am tricking him lovely."

"What did you give him for the pigs?"

"Twelve fine horses," said Huw. "With gold saddles and gold bridles! And twelve champion greyhounds, with gold collars and gold leashes!"

Huw staggered with his laughter.

"You did that swap for a few greasy pigs?" said Roger.

Huw cackled, showing his teeth, and grabbed Roger's arm for support.

"You're mad," said Roger. "You're mad. You're really mad."

"No, no," said Huw. He wiped his eyes. "I am tricking him!"

"Then I'm mad," said Roger. "Mad for listening to you."

"No, no," said Huw. "You see – them greyhounds, and the horses, and the trappings and all – I was making them out of toadstools!"

Chapter Ten

Towards the end of dinner Gwyn stacked the plates in the hatch and then went to light the fire in the sitting-room. He fiddled with paper and twigs and fed them strips of birch bark. Then he rearranged the logs in the basket by the hearth. Then he lit the lamps. He propped more wood against the fire back, trying not to send smoke into the room.

Roger and his father came through from the dining-room and settled themselves in easy chairs. Gwyn put the hanging lamp on the chimney. He had to work it gently into place inside its shade so that the asbestos mantle would not break. He kept the wick low to warm the glass. Then he rearranged the logs in the basket and brushed the hearth. He turned the lamps up slowly in case they flared.

Then he put more wood on the fire and rearranged the logs.

"I think we're suited now," said Clive. "Thanks a lot."

"I'll make sure the lamps are right, Mr Bradley," said Gwyn.

"They look fine to me," said Clive.

"And I'd better bring you some logs."

"We'll manage," said Clive. "I'd toddle along now, if I were you."

"Oh – Yes—"

"Good night, Gwyn."

"—Good night, Mr Bradley."

"One small point, old son."

"Yes, Mr Bradley?"

"If you've anything you want to tell my daughter, let's all hear it, shall we? Let's have the brussels sprouts served straight, without notes inside them, eh?"

Gwyn stood in the dark at the foot of the stairs between the dining-room and the sitting-room. He dragged his fist against the wall, trying to hurt himself.

"Had any luck with the snaps?" he heard Clive say through the open door.

"I don't know," said Roger. "I'll see tomorrow when I develop them. If they come out it'll be no thanks to that Halfbacon moron. He was trying to louse it up all the time. Honest, Dad, you'll have to do something about him. What I was telling you—"

"Yes, I know," said Clive. "But he's harmless."

"Is he, though?" said Roger. "He's as strong as an ox. And he's a real nutter."

"Yes, but he's been here all his life: he knows the ropes. And where would we find anyone for the job? The place would go to pot."

"I'd not lose sleep over that," said Roger.

"And there's Margaret, too," said Clive. "She wouldn't have much of a holiday if we had to go scrounging for a new man."

"Of course," said Roger. "I was forgetting Margaret."

Gwyn stepped back into the shadow as someone came down the stairs. It was Alison. She carried a small lamp, and when she reached the bottom of the stairs Gwyn moved forward so that she could see him. He waved towards the dining-room. Alison hesitated. She looked at the open sitting-room door. Clive and Roger were still talking. She looked at Gwyn, and again at the doorway, and then Gwyn watched her pass by him, within a yard of him, into the sitting-room, and watched her close the door.

"Hello, old stick," said Clive. He rose when Alison came in. "Now where is it? Aha. Here's a little nonsense I picked up in town today. Thought it might amuse the lady. And I managed to get you your tracing paper, by the way."

"Oh Clive, how sweet," said Alison. She took the box. "You are a darling."

Gwyn ran through the dining-room and the lamp-room to the kitchen, and stopped when he came up against the sink. He stood still. Then he turned the taps on, and leant with his hands flat against the sink and watched the water rise. He squirted some detergent into the sink, picked a dirty wineglass from the draining board, and began, slowly, methodically, to wash up. Then he dried everything and put it away. He made hardly any sound from start to finish and it was only when he went to hang the cloth to dry that he noticed his mother by the stove.

She sat on a kitchen chair, gazing at the closed firedoor. One hand gripped the towel rail, her wrist flexed as if she was trying to unscrew the rail, but her fingers slipped on the bright steel.

"Hello, Mam," said Gwyn. "Didn't see you there. Shall I light another lamp?"

"No, boy," said Nancy. "Leave it."

"Not like our own fire at Aber," said Gwyn. "Is it, Mam?"

"I should never have come," said Nancy. "I shouldn't have come. It's not right. Never go back, boy. Never go back."

"What's the matter, Mam? Got a bad head?" said Gwyn. He could not see her eyes, but he heard the rasp of her breath that was as close as she ever came to tears.

"If there was justice in Heaven," said Nancy.

Gwyn put his arm round his mother's shoulder.

"What's wrong, Mam?"

"I shouldn't have come."

"Then why did we?" said Gwyn. "How did they find our address?"

"He gave it her. Then she wrote."

"We still needn't have come."

"It's good money, boy," said Nancy. "But I should never have listened to her soft soap."

"Who had our address?" said Gwyn.

"That idiot outside."

"Huw? Why should he have it?"

Nancy's hand worked on the rail.

"Mam," said Gwyn. "Listen, Mam. We got to talk about it."

"There isn't nothing to talk about."

"Yes there is. Listen, Mam: just once. Please."

"I told you not to have anything to do with him. I mean it."

"Mam: just listen – Please, Mam!"

Nancy was silent.

"You told me so much about the valley," said Gwyn, "it was like coming home. All my life I've known this place better than Aber. Mam, I even know who people are when I see them, you described them that good! So why didn't I know about Huw Halfbacon?"

"He don't count," said Nancy.

"Yes he does," said Gwyn. "People in the valley don't call him a fool. He's important. Why haven't you told me?"

"Who you been listening to?" said Nancy. "You been talking behind my back, have you?"

"No, Mam," said Gwyn.

"You on their side, are you?" said Nancy. "Giving my character!"

"Mam!"

Gwyn was standing by the kitchen table. Nancy was sitting on the chair. She had not looked away from the door of the stove since Gwyn had first spoken to her, but now both hands were on the rail.

"Mam. I got to know about Huw. And them plates."

"I'm telling you, boy," said Nancy. Her voice was slow. "If you says another word to that old fool, or if you says another word about it to me or anyone else, I walk out of this house, and you leave that school. No more for you: you start behind the counter at the Co-op."

"You can't do that," said Gwyn.

"I'm telling you, boy."

"You can't."

"It's bad enough having to bow and scrape before them in there," said Nancy. "I'll not stand it from my own flesh and blood. I've not slaved all these years in Aber so you can look down your nose at me like one of them."

"I'm a Premium Bond on legs, is that it?" said Gwyn.

Nancy went to the kitchen dresser and fumbled in one of the cupboards. "I'm telling you, boy. – Where you off now?"

"Bed. Good night."

"Where's the aspirin?" said Nancy. "I got one of my heads."

"'I have got'," said Gwyn. "'I have got one of my heads.' It's uncouth to omit the auxiliary verb. And if you want aspirin, have you tried your purse?"

CHAPTER ELEVEN

SHE'LL NOT GO through the kitchen, because Mam bolts it. She'll not go out the front, because it's two doors to unlock. So it'll be the cloakroom. Right, girlie. Don't hurry.

Gwyn stood on the high terracing of garden above the back of the house, overlooking the cloakroom. He stood against a tree by the hedge, where the road came nearest the house, passing a few yards away at roof level as it curled round the Bryn. He had been standing there for two hours. and had not moved.

You're going to come out of that door, and the only way to nab you is to watch, and keep watching, and nobody would have the patience to stand here and do that, would they? Such a bore, old stick.

At first Gwyn had thought it would be impossible. The darkness was unrelieved, and he wanted to move – only a

Chapter Eleven

few steps, and back: anything to pass the time. But he had set himself against the trunk and gradually the night separated into cloud and mountain, and trees, river and wind, and sound in leaves and grass. A stoat killed near him, but he did not move.

The moon shone.

And Gwyn began to play with time, splitting a second into minutes, and then into hours – or taking an hour and compressing it to an instant. No hurry.

His concentration was broken once, when he was alarmed by the quick drumming of hoofs, but the next moment he grinned as a motorcycle swept along the road. Its headlamp spun shadows in his face.

Kick start!

Lights moved inside the house as the family went to bed. Two lights came to rest, one room above the other. Roger and Alison. Alison's window darkened first.

Don't be impatient, girlie.

But Gwyn misjudged her. He saw the curtains part, and a smudge of face appeared. She was sitting on the window ledge. Gwyn willed himself to sink into the tree trunk. He felt that he was floodlit. But Alison was watching the reflection of Roger's light on the steep garden, and when he blew the lamp out Alison left the window.

Now let's see how good you really are, thought Gwyn, and he began to count.

It was nearly an hour, as far as he could tell, before he saw Alison's torch flash in the bedroom.

"Not bad," said Gwyn. "Not bad at all."

When Alison unlocked the cloakroom door Gwyn was above her, ready.

She went along the back of the house and past the billiard-room. Gwyn stayed well up the road. She could be making for the back drive or the wood. She was wearing trousers and an anorak and rubber-soled climbing boots.

Alison crossed the open space by the kennels. Gwyn had to let her go. He dared not start after her until she was on the path that led down from the kennels to the drive. The path was between bushes.

Gwyn gave her an extra ten seconds, but the path was dark, and he had to grope his way, and when he came on to the drive Alison had disappeared.

Gwyn swore. There was no sigh of her. Below him the wood stretched through marshland to the river, and in front was the drive, lined with trees. He ran along the whole length to the road gate, but found nothing. He ran back towards the house. If she had gone this way to the front of the house he would have heard her when she reached the gravelled part of the drive. Alison had to be in the wood. Gwyn stopped, and began to watch and listen again. Far away among the trees, deep in the marsh, he saw a light.

Gwyn moved into the wood. As soon as he left the drive he was struggling with old roots, old ditches, slime, rocks, old paths. Brambles and nettles he found by touch, and trees heeled over when he tried to steady himself, their roots adrift in the peat. The wood was reverting to swamp.

Gwyn made towards the light. Alison had stopped, and Gwyn approached very slowly. He was within a few yards of her when the light was switched off.

Now what? She can't see any better than me, so she'll still be there: dead ahead, to the left of that stump –

The light came on again, but far over to the right, almost out of his vision.

What's she playing at?

It was moving at walking pace, flickering, as though the battery was giving out. Gwyn followed.

How's she got there so fast? I didn't hear her. He listened. The river was at the back of every sound, but his ears were used to the night.

She must have flew.

He followed the light. Alison began to zigzag.

She can't know I've rumbled her. What's she up to?

And the light went out again.

Not twice you don't, girlie.

Gwyn bent low to skyline Alison. She was somewhere near the edge of the wood, and the trees were black against the silver mountain.

Now then.

But the light came on even farther away, and well inside the wood. The battery was keeping up, but the light still flickered.

Weak connection, thought Gwyn. But how're you moving so fast? What's she after? Wanting to get me flustered so she can give me the slip?

Gwyn checked that Alison had not put him on the bright screen of moonlight. Still crouching, he ran for the cover of a tree, and stood up against it.

He was beginning to enjoy the game.

Hard luck, girlie. What are you going to do now?

The light was steady.

Your move, old stick.

Gwyn's head jerked back against the tree. The light was still there, but another had appeared, a hundred feet away to the left. Two of them. And the first light now came mincing towards him.

Gwyn swirled round the trunk. There was a third pale fire behind him. He saw that they were not torches, and never had been. He stood as if bound to the tree. They were flames. They had trapped him.

If I shout no one'll hear.

The flames walked, two at a distance, casual, backwards and forwards, marking him off from the world outside the wood, while the first flame came on.

Sometimes it sank to the ground, or paused, or turned aside from Gwyn for a moment. And then it came on.

This is where Huw's old feller went mad. Get me out of here. Get me out of here.

And sometimes the flame grew tall, and wavered, like laughter.

How do I stop from going mad? He wasn't hurt, was he? He couldn't stand it: inside: in his head. Think, man! You're not a peasant! Do something! Use your loaf!

" 'The – acceleration. Acceleration of – of a free falling body – is thirty-two – thirty-two feet per second per second.' "

There were more flames. He was aware of them, but could not take his eyes off the big flame. It was moving slowly: tottering: playing with him, and coming nearer.

I shan't go mad. What did the old feller see? – Shut up! " 'The acceleration of a free falling body is thirty-two feet per second per second. Per second per second.' " It's only fire. That's all. What happened to him, though? " 'I before E, except after C'!" shouted Gwyn.

But the flame was as tall as he was, and stood before him.

"'1536, Statute of Union! 1543, Wales divided into twelve counties! Representatives sent to Westminster!

"'Matter consists of – of three – three classes of substance! An Element! A – a Compound! And a mixture! Describe an experiment!' Mam! 'Grind! Grind – together! Together – ten grammes of fused sodium acetate and fifteen grammes of soda lime! Place some of the mixture in the test-tube, Mam, and heat strongly! Then – then $NaC_2H_3O_4$ + NaOH = Na_2CO_3 + CH_1!' It does! It does! It does!"

The other flames danced.

Gwyn stopped. It was very quiet in the wood. Gwyn stared at the flame. He let go of the tree, and took a slow step forward towards the blue fire, and another step.

"CH_4," he said. "CH_4?" One atom of carbon and four atoms of hydrogen. That's – methane –. Methane!"

Gwyn jumped at the flame. He landed on his hands and

knees in water and rotten leaves, and the flame had gone.

Gwyn slashed through the mud and stamped at the nearest tongue. It disappeared.

"Methane!" Stamp. "Methane!" Splash. "Marsh gas!" Gwyn trampled the delicate veils, laughing wide-mouthed. "CH-piddling-Four!"

He fell against a dead sapling which snapped. The sharp noise brought him up. "Oh Crimond," he said. "Alison."

That's done it, that has. Thought yourself clever, didn't you waiting so patient and all? And you have to go and chuck it away when it's handed you on a plate. Ha! Plate! Two penn'orth of methane and you scream the house down. You'll be lucky if you get within a mile of them plates now – and by, won't it make a nice little story for dear little step-brother!

Gwyn headed out of the swamp. He was so angry with himself that he took no notice of the marsh gas, nor of the wood, nor of the moonlight, nor of the noise he made.

Oaf.

Peasant.

Welsh git.

"Achoo!"

He stopped on a stride.

"A-choo!"

The sneeze was near him. He listened, but he heard nothing to give him a direction.

Gwyn scanned the wood. To his right the ground was steep and very black. In front of him a raised causeway

Chapter Eleven

stretched across a pool to a gate in the boundary fence on his left. He waited for a movement to give her away. He turned his head from side to side, examining everything that lay in his arc of vision.

Got you.

She was standing under a tree at the end of the causeway, near the gate. He looked: and looked. She became clearer, standing half hidden by the dapple of leaves in the moonlight. He could see the line of her through the branches.

But has she seen me? She'll not have the plates there, and if I let on she'll act dim, and we'll be no nearer.

I'll sit you out this time, girlie. What's up? Think you heard something? Steady: if you move, I'll see you. Wait till we're nice and quiet again and you're sure nobody's after you, then it'll be safe to carry on – and I'll be behind you, Miss Alison.

"A-choo!"

Gwyn's teeth clenched. Alison had sneezed next to him, above, and a little to the right, where the wood was darkest. Gwyn made himself look.

"Stone me!" said Gwyn.

An old hen hut on iron wheels sat rotting in the marsh, and from inside the hut came a faint noise of moving crockery.

So who's by the fence?

The figure was still there at the end of the causeway, waiting under the tree, head and shoulders, and arms and the slim body, and then he saw, no less clearly, leaves and branches, thicket and moonlight, and no one waiting.

"Stone me!"

Gwyn kneaded his face with his hands and shook his head. His eyes were heavy with strain.

There was a window on the opposite side of the hut: chicken wire was nailed over it. Gwyn found the door, which had no lock, only an outside latch.

Alison was huddled over her torch, which she had propped against a stack of plates, and was cutting owls out of a roll of tracing paper. She worked quickly, discarding each owl as soon as it was finished to begin the next. The ribbed stacks surrounded her and reflected the torchlight. She rocked on her heels with concentration.

Gwyn drew back from the window.

"Alison," he said quietly. "It's Gwyn."

The light went out.

"Alison."

He ran to the door.

"Alison. It's me. Gwyn. Don't be scared."

There was no reply.

"Alison."

He opened the door. The hut was a black hole, and he could see nothing.

"Alison. Don't act daft. I want to help you. Alison, I'm coming in. Shine your torch."

"Go away."

He put his hand on the door frame.

Chapter Eleven

"Go. Away."

There was a fluttering in the darkness, like wings, but dry and hard as a rattlesnake.

"Alison, I'm coming in."

"Go. Away."

The warning, the menace of the sound terrified him — the quick ruffling of the stacked plates.

"Don't, Alison. You've got to stop."

"Go. Away."

The plates clashed. Gwyn dived.

He hit Alison with his shoulder and pinned her arms to her sides. She fought, threshing, kicking, but Gwyn held her. His head was tucked close in to her anorak out of her reach. The dinner service splintered under them. Gwyn held her until her strength was gone, and he let her cry herself to silence.

Then he felt for the torch.

"You all right, are you?" said Gwyn.

"Yes."

"Sorry if I hurt, but I had to stop you making those owls."

"Why?"

"Why?" said Gwyn. "Don't you know why?"

"I have to make them," said Alison. "I get all worked up and edgy, and its the only thing that makes me feel better."

"Better?" said Gwyn. "Or flaked out?"

"I can't explain," said Alison. "I feel I'm going to burst, and if I can trace the pattern it goes into that. I'd nearly finished. It wouldn't take long—"

"No," said Gwyn. "You leave them, and go to bed."

"I couldn't. I'm all strung up. Please let me finish them, then I'll be all right."

"How do you make things take off?" sad Gwyn. "Like the book at me, and the plate at my Mam?"

"Do I?" said Alison. "It's this feeling I'm going to burst – it's losing your temper and being frightened, only more. My body gets tighter and tighter and – and then it's as if my skin's suddenly holes like that chicken wire, and it all shoots out."

"Has it ever happened before you made the owls?"

"—No."

"Then don't you see you have to stop?"

"I can't, Gwyn. You don't know what it's like. I must finish them."

"How many are there to do?"

"I was on the last one. Please, Gwyn. Then I can sleep. I'm dead beat."

"You look it," said Gwyn. "OK. But you promise—"

"I promise," said Alison, and she picked up the scissors.

She cut round the tracing she had made from the plate. She had taken only the main outline of the pattern, without much detail, but enough for her to make the owl.

"There," she said. "That's the whole dinner service."

"I'll have the scissors, please," said Gwyn. "Thank you. Can I keep this owl?"

"Yes," said Alison. "Do what you want."

Gwyn folded the owl into his pocket.

"Now then, come on, back up the house."

He put his hand on Alison's arm. She was trembling and her teeth began to chatter.

"Come on, Alison. You're done in."

Alison clutched at his sleeve, twisting the cloth with both hands.

"I'm frightened. Help me. It's awful. You don't know. Please. Gwyn. I'm frightened. Gwyn."

"I'm here," said Gwyn. "What are you frightened of?"

"Everything," said Alison. "I feel it's – I can't tell you. It's as if—"

"You keep saying you can't tell me, and I don't know. Why not try?"

"I haven't the words," said Alison.

"Try."

"Nothing's safe any more. I don't know where I am. 'Yesterday', 'today', 'tomorrow' – they don't mean anything. I feel they're here at the same time: waiting."

"How long have you felt this?"

"I don't know."

"Since yesterday?"

"I don't know. I don't know what 'yesterday' was."

"And that's what's frightening you?"

"Not just that," said Alison. "All of me's confused the same way. I keep wanting to laugh and cry."

"Sounds dead metaphysical to me," said Gwyn.

"I knew you wouldn't understand. Gwyn, I'm

frightened. I'm frightened of what's outside."

"Outside where?" said Gwyn.

"This hut."

"What is outside this hut?"

"Everything."

"Stop that!" said Gwyn. He shook Alison. "Don't play spooks with me! It's hysterics, man! Come up the house, now, and get some sleep."

"Gwyn! No! I daren't! I'm safe here."

"You can't spend your life in a hen hut, can you?" said Gwyn. "If you let yourself go you land up paralytic. You have to get a grip. Think of cold kippers."

"Oh, Gwyn!" Alison nearly laughed.

"I mean it. It's a creepy old wood – so think of cold kippers. It's all in the mind."

Gwyn took Alison's hand, and pushed the door open with his back. He saw Alison stare past his shoulder.

"Gwyn."

"Cold kippers, remember?"

"Gwyn. Look."

The smile stuck on his face. He looked.

A column of light stood at the end of the causeway, under the tree by the gate in the boundary fence. The column was tall, and narrowed at its top and base, and ridges of flame hung like draped cloth.

Alison began to moan.

"It's OK," said Gwyn. "Alison, it's OK. It's what I was telling you."

She pulled back towards the hut. "No," she said. "Look."

"It's only marsh gas," said Gwyn. "You find it in places like this, where plants rot under water. It's harmless."

"No," said Alison.

"It's methane. You must have heard of it. It's a simple compound of carbon and hydrogen, and it's not poisonous. Come and see."

"No. You don't understand," said Alison.

"Shall I blow it out for you?" said Gwyn. "Or jump on it?"

"No! Gwyn! Please!"

"It's only marsh gas."

"It may be marsh gas," said Alison. "It doesn't matter what it is. Can't you see? It's being used!"

"All right, Alison, back we go," said Gwyn. "It'll be daylight soon. We'll sit it out, and I'll tell you about kippers, shall I?"

They sat on the floor of the hut, and Alison hid her head in Gwyn's shoulder, and he talked to her until the sun cleared the mountain. Then he had to wake her.

They stepped from the hut into rainbow dew and walked together up to the house through the midsummer dawn.

Huw Halfbacon was scratching the gravel of the drive with a rake. He pushed his cap back on his head when Gwyn and Alison appeared.

"She's come," he said.

CHAPTER TWELVE

GWYN WENT WITH Alison as far as the cloakroom door.

Huw Halfbacon was leaning on the rake, and took no notice when Gwyn came back. Gwyn walked up to him and kicked the rake away, so that Huw fell forward. Gwyn picked up the rake and carried it to the stables. One of the garage doors was unlocked, and he went in and hung the rake on the wall. He faced Huw Halfbacon, who had followed him without speaking.

"Are you on piecework?" said Gwyn. "Or is raking the drive your answer to the problem of leisure?"

"There's a lot to be done," said Huw. "And I don't have help."

"So you start at four o'clock every morning."

"Only in summer," said Huw.

"Don't put that tourist trade look on for me," said

Gwyn. "Keep the simple peasant for the other mugs, Mister Huw, not me."

Huw said nothing. Gwyn noticed that his arms were the same thickness from shoulder to wrist, and hung motionless.

"Alison's finished tracing the owls on that dinner service. She makes them into paper models." Gwyn felt in his pocket: frowned: then turned his pocket inside out. "I had one of them," he said. "Never mind. She makes these owls. Then soon after, it seems the pattern vanishes off the plates. First question, Mister Huw."

"She wants to be flowers," said Huw, "but you make her owls. Why do we destroy ourselves?"

"I'm asking the questions," said Gwyn. "What have those plates to do with Blodeuwedd?"

"She is the lady," said Huw.

"So?"

"And she has come."

"What does that mean?"

"I don't know."

"Mister Huw," said Gwyn. "I've just seen Alison so frightened she was as big an idiot as you pretend to be, and I think you know about it, and you're going to tell me. What's wrong with the plates?"

"My grandfather made them."

"So?"

"He went mad."

"Right, we'll play it your way for a bit," said Gwyn.

"Why did he go mad?"

"Down in the wood," said Huw.

"I said 'why', not 'where' – but that's nothing. Where in the wood, Mister Huw?"

"There's a causeway over the swamp to a gate in the fence on the river bank," said Huw. "He saw the lady made of flowers, but he was not strong enough to keep her, and she changed into – he would never say what happened. Down in the wood. We don't go there."

Gwyn had lost his colour. "By the gate," he said. "At the end of the causeway, under a tree, close to the hen hut."

"How do you know that?" said Huw. He bulked against the open doorway. "How do you know? We don't go there." His arms swung forward, and held Gwyn. "I've told you, we don't go there."

"Who's 'we'? You're not my boss. I'll go where I like," said Gwyn. "Lay off, you're hurting."

"We are not free," said Huw. "We have tried too many times to be free. No lord is free. My grandfather tried, my uncle tried, and I have tried to end it, but it has no end."

"Lay off!"

Gwyn twisted out of Huw's grip, but could not reach the door. He vaulted over a chest of drawers and took hold of it by the corners, ready to dodge if Huw moved. But Huw stayed in the middle of the floor, and spoke as if nothing had happened.

"She wants to be flowers, but you make her owls. You must not complain, then, if she goes hunting."

Chapter Twelve

"Talk sense, man!" cried Gwyn. "Please! I've got to know!"

"You do know," said Huw. "Lleu, Blodeuwedd and Gronw Pebyr. They are the three who suffer every time, for in them the power of this valley is contained, and through them the power is loosed."

"What's this power?" said Gwyn.

Huw did not answer.

"Huw. Is it ghosts?"

Huw shook his head.

"Is the power in the plates?"

"Some of it," said Huw. "For a while, and a while."

"And that picture in the billiard-room? You know, don't you?"

"Oh, yes," said Huw. "My uncle painted that."

"When?"

"Oh, years ago."

"But it's centuries old, man!"

"Yes, my uncle painted that."

"But he can't have done."

"And he found peace, too, that way before he died. You see. Grandfather and uncle were great men, and they thought they could tame her. They thought they could end the sorrow of this valley. But they made her owls, and she went hunting. They rid themselves at last by locking her in plate and wall – and then they sought a quiet grave."

"What's it to do with you, or your grandfather, or your uncle?" said Gwyn.

"We have the blood," said Huw. "And we must bear it. A lord must look to his people, and they must not suffer for his wrong. When I took the powers of the oak and the broom and the meadowsweet, and made them woman, that was a great wrong — to give those powers a thinking mind."

"You didn't do that," said Gwyn. "You're mixed up. It's a story, Huw, in books — about the old days, long ago, and it was a man called Gwydion who made Blodeuwedd: not you. You've got to straighten yourself out over what you know and what you've read or been told. It's a muddle inside you. You didn't make anybody out of flowers, and your uncle didn't paint that picture, for a start."

"What do I know?" said Huw, and Gwyn was frightened by the fear in Huw's eyes. "What do I know?... I know more than I know... I don't know what I know... The weight, the weight of it!"

"Huw! Stop acting simple! They think you're off your head, and Roger's trying to have you sacked. I've heard them."

"They'll not do anything," said Huw.

"They'll give you the push, all right, if it suits them," said Gwyn. "Try, man. Don't play up so — that guff about toadstools and pigs — that was another story about Gwydion, not you. Alison's been reading those old tales, and when Roger was on about you last night she came out with it. It's one thing to put on the wizened retainer act if it brings in a few quid, but this lot here think you're taking them for a ride. You'll be out on your neck. You don't own the place, man."

"Don't I?" said Huw. "Oh, their name is on the books of the law, but I own the ground, the mountain, the valley: I own the song of the cuckoo, the brambles, the berries: the dark cave is mine!"

"You won't see it, will you?" Gwyn pushed past Huw. "Out of my way, you daft devil! – And get that cover made for the trap door," he called back over his shoulder, "or else!"

CHAPTER THIRTEEN

"You're looking a bit peaky this morning," said Clive. "Sure you're OK? Mustn't overdo things, you know. Not good for a young lady."

"I'm fine, thanks," said Alison. "I'm not properly awake yet, that's what's wrong. I'm always like this if I oversleep."

"Shall I rustle up Old Nancy to do you a poached egg?" said Clive. "We kept your breakfast as long as we could, but it turned nasty."

"No. Honest, Clive, I'll be all right. I think I'll go for a breath of fresh air."

"That's the stuff," said Clive.

"Where's Roger?" said Alison.

"He's down in the cellar with his films: developing, I think. Anyway, he said not to disturb him. He's locked the door to stop us from walking in at a crucial moment – you know what these darkroom fanatics are."

"Never mind," said Alison. "I shan't be long."

"Um – remember what Margaret said, won't you?"

"Yes, Clive."

"Mothers can't help worrying—"

"No, Clive."

"I mean, she has your best interests at heart—"

"Yes, Clive."

"She – we want you to enjoy yourself, you know. We want you to be happy, that's all."

"You're very sweet, Clive," said Alison. "See you at lunch."

"Cheers," said Clive.

Alison walked along the river path below the terrace. The heat of the day was already uncomfortable, but under the trees the air was still cool.

The path went into the marsh at the hen hut. Gwyn was sitting on a stump by the path.

"Hello," said Alison.

"Hello."

Alison climbed on to a rock.

Gwyn pointed through the trees. "See that dark line going up the mountain?" he said. "That's the old peat road. Every summer the people from the valley went up the top to cut peat. Four days it took them."

"How did they carry it down?" said Alison.

"Horses," said Gwyn.

"But it's so steep."

"They used sledges. And see that scar above the stream

there? That was the quarry for building the house. All the good slate is that side of the river: over this side it's very poor stone. Have a look at the road bridge next time you go to the shop. It was made of the bad slate, and it's falling to bits. But the house is like new. It'll never wear out."

"I wish I was like you," said Alison. "You belong here."

"Me? This is the first time I've seen the place—"

"That's it," said Alison. "You came a week ago, and you know everything as if you'd always lived here – while I've been spending holidays at the house all my life, and yet I don't belong. I'm as useless as one of those girls in fashion photographs – just stuck in a field of wheat, or a puddle, or on a mountain, and they look gorgeous but they don't know where they are. I'm like that. I don't belong."

"It's your house," said Gwyn.

"That doesn't count for much at the moment."

"How long has your family owned the place?"

"I've no idea. Daddy inherited from a cousin who was killed."

"When was he killed?"

"Ooh, ages ago: before I was born. I've seen pictures of him – he was very good-looking. His name was Bertram."

"But it is your house."

"—Yes."

"If you really put your foot down, would you have your own way?"

"Mummy and Clive run the estate now. It's not easy. Why? What's the matter?"

Chapter Thirteen

"I'm worried about Huw," said Gwyn. "You won't sack him, will you?"

"They're talking about it," said Alison. "But there's no one to take his place. Clive's bothered about him being dangerous. Is he?"

Gwyn shook his head. "I don't know. There's too much that's screwy with him — and too much of it is sense. He talks so elliptical, even in Welsh, you just can't make him out. I'm feeling bad about it, I suppose, because we had a set to after you went in, and I lost my temper. But now I've been thinking, and what he says could be true."

"What's that?"

"Come and look in the hen hut," said Gwyn.

"I'd rather not," said Alison. "I've been thinking, too."

"It won't take a moment," said Gwyn. He opened the door. "There. One dinner service, plain white, smashed: ready for instant disposal. What am I offered?"

"No, Gwyn. I'm scared again. And the tight feeling inside."

"Don't worry. The pattern's gone and every piece is bust. You can tell yourself we broke it when we were scrapping last night, if you like. I don't know how you cope with the pattern. And where are the owls you made?"

"Gwyn, don't go on at me, please! Not you. You're the only one I can talk to."

"You wouldn't think it," said Gwyn. "What about when I needed to talk to you? — The way you swept past and went in: 'Oh, Clive, how sweet!' — and me out there. How do you think that felt?"

"I had to," said Alison. "Mummy was coming down any second, and we'd had the most awful row about that message you put in the sprouts."

"Well, so what?" said Gwyn.

"Saying you had to see me. Mummy was livid. She said some hateful things. I didn't know she could be like that."

"Like what?"

"I can't tell you, Gwyn."

"Thank you very much, Miss Alison. I'm sorry I spoke."

"Don't, Gwyn. It's not me."

"Who is it, then?"

"I—Well—"

"I only want to talk to you, girl."

"Me too. You're the only one who's ever called me 'Alison'."

"That's your name."

"But I'm always called 'Ali'. It's horrid. Ali Alleycat."

"I just want to talk to you," said Gwyn. "With you it all goes how I mean it. Have you had your breakfast?"

"No, I couldn't."

"Neither could I. It was like sawdust. I couldn't swallow."

Gwyn went back to the tree stump.

"We must talk about these plates."

"Why?" said Alison. "They're broken. I don't care two hoots – oh! Two hoots!" Alison laughed, covering her face with her hands. "Two hoots!"

"Steady," said Gwyn. "Come on, Alison, that's enough now. Come on, girl. I'm sorry. I should have thought."

Chapter Thirteen

"Hello," said Roger. He was leaning against a tree. "I wondered where you were. I've been shouting after you. I've some prints I want you to see."

"In a minute," said Gwyn.

"Come and see, Ali," said Roger.

"I told you in a minute," said Gwyn.

"Ali," said Roger. "Your mother's knocking around. Don't you think—? Remember?"

"What's he on about?" said Gwyn.

Alison looked at him. "Gwyn – don't come to the house with us. Gwyn, I tried: but Mummy said I wasn't to talk to you."

"It's quite in order, Miss Alison," said Gwyn. "And I'll use the tradesman's entrance in future." He walked briskly along the path and then up through the wood towards the back drive.

"Gwyn, I daren't!"

"That fellow's got a chip on his shoulder a mile high," said Roger.

CHAPTER FOURTEEN

"OF COURSE IF I'd had the proper stuff: I could have blown it up as big as the wall," said Roger. "As it is, I've been sweating in that cellar all morning trying to balance out, but it's murder to use that film and paper for really detailed work. Still, there's enough to give you some idea, and perhaps you'll be able to tell what it is: a fresh eye, and all that."

"Not now, Roger," said Alison.

"The prints are on the dining-room table. They'll be a bit damp, so mind you don't flap them about."

"No. Later. Not now."

"Didn't half give me a shock at first, I'll tell you," said Roger. "It's the last two, when that great hairy Welsh freak was watching. Gwyn was there when I took most of the others. You can see his hand. He was sitting on the stone before he went off to find his mate. But the point is, Ali, the pictures were all taken within five minutes, once I'd set the camera up, and I was looking at the Bryn pretty well all the time. Anyway, see for yourself. They're in here."

But as soon as Roger opened the door Alison ran past him and up the stairs.

"Oy! Ali!"

Her door banged and he heard a muffled chime of bed springs.

"Women!" said Roger, and went into the dining-room. His photographs were piled on the windowsill in full sunlight. The top prints had rolled themselves into tubes. Nancy was laying the table.

"Who's moved my prints?" said Roger.

"They was on the table," said Nancy.

"I know they were on the table. I put them there to finish drying. "I've spent all morning on those prints!"

"They was in the way," said Nancy. "I got work to do, and dining-room table isn't the place for sticky paper when you has to polish it every day and sometimes twice."

"In the way?" said Roger. "You've ruined my prints, that's all! In the way? Is it your job to decide what's in the way here?"

"I wishes to see Mrs Bradley," said Nancy.

"You'll not interfere with stuff that doesn't concern you, that's what you'll do."

"Hello, hello, hello," said Clive. He began to talk while he was still coming in through the cloakroom. "What's all the hoo-ha?"

"I wants to speak to Missis," said Nancy. "I'm giving notice."

"She went and ruined—"

"All right, all right," said Clive. "Let's drop the temperature, shall we? Now then, old son, collect your tackle and scarper, eh?"

"But Dad—"

"I'll help you sort it out in the parlour, but wait a tick, there's a good lad. I'll be right with you."

Roger picked up the photographs and left the room. He went through to the parlour and unrolled the sheets on the floor, and listened to the voices – Nancy's monotone, and his father's persuasiveness – then Clive came back into the parlour. He was putting his wallet back in his pocket. "Expensive holiday, this," he said.

"I was all morning with these prints," said Roger, "and she's messed them up."

"Easy does it. You'll not go far if you don't learn to bend with the wind, and Nance is blowing a bit strong lately."

Roger spread out the photographs, weighting them at the corners with ornaments. "Well, actually, it's not as bad as I thought," he said. "If I can keep them flat now they may be OK. Sorry I flew off the handle, Dad: it was the way she slung them about. Couldn't she see they were there on purpose?"

"She wouldn't think," said Clive. "You mustn't expect the Nancys of this world to have too much savvy."

"Gwyn seems pretty smart."

"Ah yes: well: that's the trouble: barrack-room lawyers we called them in the RAF. They're the worst. But brains aren't everything, by a long chalk. You must have the background."

"Is that why Margaret's gone so County with Alison?"

"Tricky," said Clive. "Very, very tricky – um – you know? Now what about these snaps of yours? Shall we put them on the billiard table? It's better than in here, and we'll anchor them with snooker balls. Not come out too well, have they? What's this, a wet weekend in Brum?"

"You tell me," said Roger. "I'll put them in order. Now here's the straightforward seven shots of that stone by the river. In the first three you can see Gwyn's hand – he was sitting on top of the stone. Right. Now here are enlargements of the middle part of each picture. They're all the same – the different shades are because I gave them different exposures – but you can see how I've made the hole frame the trees on the Bryn."

"Yes, jolly good," said Clive. "Quite effective."

"Now in the last two pictures Gwyn wasn't there. But old Streakybacon had turned up and was making snide remarks. Here."

"Jolly good: spot on again."

"Are they?" said Roger.

Clive knelt over the prints and looked closely at them, comparing the two sets. "Aha," he said. "Yes."

"What, Dad?"

"In these last two there's something just inside the trees – between those on the left."

"What is it?"

"Um – ah. Can't say. It's not on the others, right enough. Have you tried a magnifying glass?"

"No, but I've enlarged the enlargement. Now look at these."

Roger showed his father another seven prints, enlarged so that none of the Stone of Gronw appeared, only the trees on the Bryn.

"There's the three with Gwyn, there's two after he'd gone, and there's the two when Halfbacon was watching."

"No doubt about it now, is there?" said Clive. "There's something extra in the last two."

"What is it?"

Clive put on his glasses. "—No," he said. "No go. If you made it bigger we might see."

"I have," said Roger. "Here's your wet weekend."

The prints were coarse patterns of blobs and lines.

"What's gone wrong?" said Clive.

"It's the film and the paper," said Roger. "You can only blow the negative up so far, and then the grain of the film starts to show, and the colour definition separates into black and white, so you're left with patches of each, and nothing in between. If you do it deliberately it can be a kind of abstract."

"Yes—?" said Clive.

"I've tried to compromise," said Roger, and he pointed

to another row of prints. "Here. I've taken it as far as possible and stopped just before the picture disintegrates. What do you make of it? Again, the shading's different because they're two different exposures."

The trees in the picture were like burnt match sticks, and between two of them was a cluster of grey and black beads.

"I'd say this was someone on a horse, either lifting a pole up, or waving his hand."

"Have you seen any horses since we came here?" said Roger. "The farms use tractors."

"It's a bit on the small side, I must admit," said Clive. "I tell you what, though: it could be a pony. Pony trekking's very popular nowadays."

"What's on his head?"

"Ah – nothing?"

"His hair's long, then," said Roger. "Gathered at the back and down to his shoulders."

"One of these beatnik types," said Clive. "I must say, it's not often you see them in the great outdoors, is it?"

"Look at the next print," said Roger. "It's underexposed. That's why it's so much darker, and the blobs have run together more."

"He's taken his hand down," said Clive, "but you can't see much of him, can you? Wait a minute – that pony's a bit round fore and aft."

"It may have dropped its head," said Roger.

"True. But if I hadn't known about the other photo I'd say it was a motorbike."

"Up there?"

"Just the place for a scramble, though I think we'd have heard more about it, don't you? Was there anyone riding round?"

"No, Dad. That's the point. The pictures were all shot within five minutes, and I was watching the Bryn. How have these two turned out like this?"

"I haven't the faintest: unless Halfbacon was putting a jinx on you."

"Are you serious, Dad? Could he?"

"Could he what?"

"Put a jinx on me."

"Now steady," said Clive. "We're not in the Middle Ages: you'll be roasting the chap at the stake next."

Roger and his father gathered up the prints and carried them to the billiard-room. The door was open, but they could not go in, because a wheelbarrow was blocking the way. The wheelbarrow held broken pebble-dash and Gwyn was clearing the last of it from the floor with a brush and shovel.

Roger and his father waited outside. Gwyn said nothing, but went on with his sweeping. "I'd forgotten," said Roger. "There's something to show you." They waited.

"We'll settle for that, old lad," said Clive. "Chop-chop."

"I was brushing up, like," said Gwyn. "You don't want this rubbish here, isn't it?"

"Shift your barrow, will you, so we can get in."

"That's right, Mr Bradley," said Gwyn, and went on sweeping.

Chapter Fourteen

"The barrow, laddie," said Clive. "Smartish."

"Yes, sir," said Gwyn. He worked a fragment of plaster towards the shovel, holding the broom in his other hand, close to the head. He followed the plaster round the billiard table and trapped it against one of the legs. He swung the shovel up, carried it to the barrow, and dropped the plaster in. "At once, sir."

Gwyn pushed the barrow through the doorway and bumped it down the steps to the path at the back of the house.

"Dumb Insolence, as near as a toucher!" said Clive.

"Never mind, Dad. Come and see this." Roger put his photographs on the billiard table. "What do you think of our mural? – Oh, Dad!"

He was looking at a bare wooden panel.

"The vindictive beggar! He's scraped it off!" Roger ran to the steps. Gwyn was wheeling the barrow. "Hey! You! Gwyn stopped. "Come here!" Roger jumped the steps. "What did you have to wreck that painting for, you Welsh oaf?"

"Master Roger," said Gwyn, "there's asking for a poke in the gob you are, indeed to goodness, look you."

CHAPTER FIFTEEN

WHEN SHE HEARD the shouting Alison rolled off her bed and went to the window. It was Roger's voice. She opened the fanlight. Gwyn appeared below the window, wheeling a barrow towards the stables.

The sun had warmed the ledge. Alison leant her head against the glass. Some distance away the long stone fish tank by the lawn sparked where the inlet broke from the ferns, and she saw herself mirrored among haloes that the sun made on the water. The brightness destroyed the image of the house, so that all she saw was her face.

I'm up here, and down there, thought Alison. Which is me? Am I the reflection in the window of me down there?

Gwyn came back from the stables. He was walking with his shoulders hunched, and he kicked at every pebble. He sat on the edge of the tank, right next to the Alison in the water: he seemed to be watching her.

Now am I here, and you there? Or are we together? If I'm the reflection here then we'll be able to talk to each other. "Hello, Gwyn."

Gwyn said nothing. He reached out to touch her hair, and she was at once gold and whiteness over the water, and Alison was back in the window and the metal frame was hurting her cheek. And Gwyn looked up.

He had not expected to see her. He had been fighting his anger all the way to the rubbish dump and back. The water was calm, and he tried to slip his hand into the stillness without breaking the clear light, but ripples sprang from his fingers. He looked up.

Alison was in the window. She did not move. The stillness he had tried to enter was now all round him, and Gwyn sat, and watched. But the gong sounded for lunch, and Alison hurried downstairs, while Gwyn went to drain the potatoes and put them in their dish in the serving hatch.

"What you been up to?" said Nancy after the first course. "He says you're not to wait on at table today."

"I offered to thump his son and heir a few minutes ago," said Gwyn.

"What for?"

"Being personal."

"Did you hit him?"

"No. Daddy broke it up."

"Pity," said Nancy, and carried the cheese board through to the dining-room.

Gwyn frowned after his mother. Pity? Then he cleared the dirty plates from the hatch and stacked them at the sink. His hands trembled at the idea. There was time, but he had to be quick, and quiet.

Five boxes. Two from each wouldn't be missed.

He tried the sitting-room first. One box. He opened it, and it was full: at least a hundred cigarettes. He took ten straight away, but that was too many, and he fed them back until the box looked full again. He had five cigarettes left in his hand.

Gwyn went into the parlour, and found two boxes, but the first he opened was nearly empty and he dared not take any. Three from the second box.

More: more. But there were no more boxes, and knives were clinking in the hatch. He ran to the kitchen and started to wash up as his mother brought the cutlery in. She took the coffee to the dining-room.

Minutes. Gwyn dried his hands, trying to make an inventory of the house in his head, but no boxes showed themselves. Eight cigarettes were as bad as none.

Gwyn went back to the sitting-room and looked behind the cushions on the chairs and found nothing. There was time for only one try. He stepped into the cloakroom, and put his hand in the pocket of Clive's fishing jacket.

This is where the light always goes on, thought Gwyn, but nothing happened, and his fingers gripped a flat metal box.

Back in the kitchen Gwyn put the ten cigarettes in a

drawer. One was bent, but he had not time to straighten it. He opened the kitchen door to the outside passage, took the lids off the dustbins, and began to turn the contents over.

Then Gwyn finished washing up. He came down from his bedroom a quarter of an hour later. Nancy sat by the stove, drinking the remains of the coffee.

"Where you been, boy?" she said. "You was clumping about no end."

"Upstairs, Mam." Gwyn pulled a chair to the stove. "Mam," he said. "I'm sorry about last night. That was a rotten trick with your purse. I bought you a present, see." He held out a cigarette packet. "I couldn't get your usual. Will these do?"

Nancy took the packet. Unless she noticed the wet stains from the tea leaves in the dustbin; if he had managed to fold the silver paper tightly; if the bent cigarette was not the first she picked—

"Mm," said Nancy. "All right, boy." She twisted a spill of newspaper and lit it from the stove. "Mm. They'll do. Where you find the money?"

"I've been saving a bit," said Gwyn.

"I thought you was coming it yesterday," said Nancy.

"Mam, if I'd belted Roger what would have happened? Would we have been sacked?"

"Depends how hard, doesn't it?"

"You wouldn't mind if I belted him?"

"Him? Ha! 'Oh,' he says. 'Where's my photos?' he says. 'Who's moved them off the table? You got no right,' he says.

'Don't you touch anything without permission,' he says. And there was all that sticky on my table I just polished. And then he comes in and thinks he can flash his pound notes around."

"Who?"

"Him. Lord Muck."

"Mr Bradley?"

" 'Mr Bradley'! When I think of the titled heads I've seen in that dining-room—! He's not even a gentleman!"

"How do you know he isn't?" said Gwyn.

"There's ways of catching them," said Nancy. "And when he was flashing his pound notes, I thought, right, I thought, if there was justice in Heaven there'd be others with cheque books. I'll lay knife and fork, and we'll see how you manages a pear, my laddo."

"A pear, Mam?"

"It takes a gentleman to eat a pear proper," said Nancy. "He had it on the floor in no time – oh, I made him look a fool!" Nancy coughed at her cigarette.

"What happened then?"

"That Alison covered for him. She picked hers up and ate it in her hand, but she knew. She knew. She's a twicer, that one."

Nancy pulled on her cigarette, and her eyes narrowed. Gwyn said nothing. When his mother did this she was living in her memories: it was her x-ray look. "Yes," she said. "If we all had our rights there'd be others with cheque books. My Bertram could eat a pear lovely."

Chapter Fifteen

Gwyn held his breath and tried not to move, but his mother continued to focus on a point six feet through the stove and the wall behind it.

"Yes, Mam?"

"What, boy?"

"Oh – sorry, Mam."

"You done that job yet?" said Nancy.

"What job?"

"That trap door."

"Yes, Mam, after breakfast, soon as Alison got up."

"Show me," said Nancy.

They went upstairs to Alison's room, knocked, and went in.

"I done it properly, see, Mam," said Gwyn. "Brass screws. That all right now?"

"Yes, you done that." Nancy sat on the bed and put her head on the rail. "Brass screws for coffins," she said.

"Yes, Mam."

"You don't know, boy. Them plates was for my bottom drawer. Not that I needed no bottom drawer, but he says, 'You have them for your bottom drawer,' he says, 'and let them think what they like.' My Bertram didn't care that much." Nancy tried to snap her fingers. "We'd be married, he said: he didn't care. 'Hang the lot of them,' he says. 'If they don't like it they know what they can do.' But he didn't know what they could do, boy."

"What, Mam?"

"If there was justice in Heaven," said Nancy, "I should be

sitting at that table today saying potatoes was cold, not them. But he didn't know what they could do."

"What, Mam?"

"That jealous idiot outside," said Nancy. "That mad fool. Oh, it was accident, of course. They said." She went to the window and threw her cigarette out of the fanlight. "But there isn't the pound notes in London to pay me for losing my Mr Bertram, just when I had him landed, high and dry."

CHAPTER SIXTEEN

ROGER WAS SETTING up his tripod again on the bank. Alison sat in the shade of the Stone of Gronw among the meadowsweet. Clive stood in the river.

"You're wrong," said Alison. "Gwyn wouldn't do it. I know he has a temper, but he wouldn't deliberately spoil that painting out of spite."

"Wouldn't he? You've not seen him when he's vicious," said Roger. "He'd do anything. I could tell you—"

"Don't bother," said Alison. "Are you really going to spend all day clicking that thing? I want to go up the mountain."

"You're not interested in my prints, so why worry?"

"It's stifling here: and these flowers are going to make me sneeze if I stay. There'll be some wind at the top."

"As long as you don't melt on the way up."

"Cut out the bickering, you two," said Clive. "No wonder I'm not catching any fish."

"I want to go up the mountain, Clive," said Alison, "and Roger just wants to waste his film."

"You know what they say – one man's whatsit."

"I want to go up the peat road," said Alison. "You can't see much of it from here, but it's the snaky line on the side of the mountain. They used to cut peat on the top and bring it down with sledges."

"Did they, now?" said Clive.

"Yes. They used horses. It took four days every year."

"How do you know?" said Roger.

"This isn't my first visit, even if it's yours," said Alison. "I've been coming here all my life."

"Then you can find your own way up the fascinating peat road, can't you?"

"For crying out loud!" said Clive. "Look, Ali, if you want to go, go: but stay on this road thing of yours, won't you? Mountains can be tricky."

"Will you come, Clive?"

"Not after Nancy's spuds, thanks. And I know the fish don't seem to be around, but I doubt if they've taken to the hills yet."

Alison went along the river bank to a track that led up the mountain from the ford. The track followed the line of a stream between hedgerows to a stone barn and a sheep dip, then it rose above the stream, and Alison was on the mountain. The fields lay below her, and she was among

Chapter Sixteen

bracken fronds, and boulders of white quartz, and flowering thorn.

The track was the peat road, now a sunken line on the mountain, and she climbed the bend that she had seen from the river. Already Roger and Clive were no more than spots of colour, and soon she was round the shoulder and the house was hidden.

Alison rested on a slate outcrop. The peat road went up a fold in the mountain made by the stream, but led away from the water. She was very hot.

Now that the house was out of sight there was nothing to tell her where she was, and her fear brushed against her.

Cold kippers.

It works! Cold, cold, cold kippers! Still: nothing changes here. Rocks and bracken. It could be a thousand years ago. Cold kippers.

Alison thought of turning back. Don't be silly. It's only this bit. Higher up I'll be able to see the whole valley. And the sheep are all right, with patches of dye on their fleece. That's modern.

Is it?

Is it?

Alison looked at the cliffs above her, each with its trail of frost-broken slate down the hillside. Something moved: dark: not a sheep.

Alison screamed, but there was a clatter of stones across her path and the way was blocked by a figure standing against the sun.

"It's OK, girl."

"Oh, Gwyn!"

He was panting. "What's up? Expecting bows and arrows and two coats of quick non-drying woad, were you?"

"Yes! Almost!" Alison laughed. "I am stupid!"

"You can say that again. By, but you're a fast climber."

"How did you know I was here?"

"I was listening to your idyll back there. All I had to do was get to the ford and race you along the stream, then hide here before you. That's all." Gwyn dragged up a length of moss and squeezed it on his brow. "I do it every morning before breakfast, and twice on Sundays."

"Gwyn, we mustn't."

"Mustn't what?"

"Talk like this."

"Like what?"

"We mustn't talk at all."

Gwyn stuffed the moss between his teeth, and crossed his eyes.

"Gwyn, please don't fool about. Oh, you know we mustn't see each other."

"Why not? You in quarantine for smallpox, are you?"

"You know Mummy says I mustn't talk to you."

Gwyn gazed at the crags, and slowly followed them to the next hillside, and down to the valley, to the mountain on the other side of the valley, and straight up to the sky.

"I can't see her," he said.

"Gwyn," said Alison, "I'm going home."

"Right," said Gwyn, "I'll come with you."

"No!"

"Why not?"

"Don't! Please! What do you want?"

"I want you to be yourself, for a change," said Gwyn. "That's what I want. Let's climb this metamorphic Welsh mountain."

"Mummy'll be so angry if she finds out, and I hate upsetting her."

"That's the all-year-round cultural pursuit in your family," said Gwyn. "Not Upsetting Mummy."

"Don't talk like that."

"You're not having much luck with it, though, are you? Mummy was upset yesterday, and Mummy was upset the day before, and I bet you anything Mummy will be upset today. I wonder what pleasures tomorrow will bring.— And your stepfather's in trouble with my Mam, isn't he? He'll find it tough going there. She's the blue on armour plating."

"Why are you so horrid about people?" said Alison.

"My Mam, you mean? She hates my guts."

"She doesn't!"

"A lot you know," said Gwyn. "What are you wanting to do when you leave school, Alison?"

"Mummy wants me to go abroad for a year."

"But what do you want to do?"

"I've not thought. I expect I'll go abroad."

"Then what? Sit at home and arrange flowers for Mummy?"

"Probably."

"And Roger?"

"He'll join Clive in his business, I expect."

"Real fireballs, aren't you?" said Gwyn. "Straining like greyhounds at the slips."

"What's wrong with that?"

"Nothing. Nothing. I don't blame you, girl."

"What are you going to do, then, that's so marvellous?"

Gwyn was silent.

"Gwyn?"

"What?"

"I'm not laughing at you."

"At Aber," said Gwyn, "they want me to go on."

"On what?"

"With school."

"I can see you in about thirty years," said Alison. "You'll be Professor of Welsh!"

"Not me. I've got to get out of this place. There's nothing here but sheep."

"I thought it meant a lot to you," said Alison.

"It does. But you can't eat a feeling."

"What will you do?"

"At the moment the likely chance is I'll be behind a shop counter in a couple of months."

"Oh no!"

"Oh yes!"

"Why?"

"My Mam thinks it's a good idea."

"But she must have worked to see you through school," said Alison. "Why throw it away?"

"Mam's ambitious," said Gwyn. "But her horizon's about three inches high. As long as I leave the house in a suit every morning, that's Mam happy. The other lads in our street wear overalls."

"Oh, the stupid woman!"

"Now who's being horrid?" said Gwyn.

They climbed for a while without talking.

"I didn't know this could happen," said Alison. "Everything with me has been easy—"

"Well, don't start feeling guilty about it," said Gwyn. "It's not your fault."

"What will you do if she makes you leave?"

"I've got plans," said Gwyn.

They were on top of the mountain. Before them stretched a plateau slashed with colour, reds and blacks and blues and browns and greens rolling into the heat. Gwyn and Alison made for a cairn on a hillock, which was the only point in all the landscape. It was farther away than it looked.

"If it was a clear day," said Alison, "how far could we see?"

"I don't know that one," said Gwyn. "But this cairn is the county boundary."

"The valley's disappeared," said Alison.

"It's the plateau. That's what does it. It's the same height either side, so you can't tell what's a valley and what's a dip in the grass until you're there."

They sat with their backs against the cairn. In front of them at the foot of the hillock was a dark level of water in a peat bed.

"When you were by the tank before lunch," said Alison, "could you see me in the water?"

"No."

"From where I sat it was as if we were right next to each other, like we are now, and you were watching me."

"I didn't think you were anywhere near until I saw you in the window."

"You put your hand in the water and touched my hair, and then the ripples broke it up."

"Fancy that," said Gwyn. "—Yes: fancy that! Alison? How far would you say it is from the tank to the window?"

"About ten yards. Why?"

"Father than this peat hollow is from the cairn, anyway," said Gwyn, "and not much higher. Stand up."

Alison stood.

"Can you see yourself?"

"No."

"Can you see me?"

"No."

"Tell me when you can." Gwyn walked down to the water. He was on the edge of the pool, and bending forward, when Alison called out.

"How is it compared with your reflection this morning?" said Gwyn.

"About the same size."

"Same size?"

"Yes: I told you it looked as if we were next to each other."

"Done any Physics, have you?"

"A bit."

"Then you'll know, won't you? – 'The image of an object in a mirror appears to be as far behind the mirror as the object is in front.' "

"Well?"

"So if you could see yourself in the fish tank you'd look as if you were twenty yards away – twice as far as you really were."

"Well?"

"So you wouldn't look as big as me. So the angles were all wrong anyhow for you to see your reflection. So it wasn't your reflection. It couldn't have been, unless you were standing on the edge of the tank."

"The water was glittery," said Alison, "but I could tell it was me – my colour of hair, and face, and – well, it just was."

"You saw a blonde reflected in the water," said Gwyn. "Her hair came down either side of her face and she was fair-skinned. That's all you can be sure of."

"You're confusing me," said Alison. "I was trying to tell you about feeling happy, and you go and make it all ordinary with your angles and mirrors."

"Ordinary? Girl, you can't be that stupid! Wake up! You saw the woman in the picture! You saw Blodeuwedd!"

"No, no, no, no, no, no, no, no—" Alison turned her face to the rocks of the cairn. "Don't talk like that. It must have been me reflected in the glass – in the window. Help me, Gwyn."

"I want to help you, but you don't help me," said Gwyn. "This thing won't go away if you shut your eyes, Alison. Come along and I'll show you."

Gwyn set off across the plateau. Alison held on to the cairn as if to a lifebuoy, but as Gwyn drew father away and merged into the sun haze she plunged after him through the bog.

"Good girl."

"I'm not a poodle," said Alison.

"That's better," said Gwyn.

They laughed.

"Did you scrape the painting off?" said Alison.

"Did you scrape the pattern?" said Gwyn.

The water was behind them, and parched grass lay like bloom on the mountain.

"It's so big," said Alison. "All the things that seem important don't matter up here. It's so big."

"Remember that, then," said Gwyn.

"Mountains and cold kippers?"

Gwyn and Alison laughed again.

"Your stepbrother's a right charmer," said Gwyn.

"It's only Roger's way," said Alison, "and he feels dreadful about it afterwards. He's had a pretty rough time. His mother walked out, you know, and Mummy says it was in all the papers. Mummy calls her 'The Birmingham Belle'."

"Nice lady, your Mam," said Gwyn. "How does Roger take that?"

"She never says it in front of Roger – not on purpose. He was very fond of his mother."

"Yes, he is touchy," said Gwyn. "By, I wish mine would flit."

"Why are you so brittle?" said Alison.

"Me?" said Gwyn. "The three of us are lame ducks, by the sound of it. My legs snap easy, that's all." He started to waddle with a limp.

"Gwyn! You're impossible!"

"Quack," said Gwyn.

"Where are we going? I mustn't be late."

"Your sense of direction's not much good, girl. We're making for the valley, but farther along from the peat road. You can see the valley opening up now, can't you? Head for that rock straight in front."

"Why? What is it?"

"The Ravenstone. You'll see."

The plateau dipped to the outcrop, and then –

"Gosh!" said Alison.

The Ravenstone was a mass of vertical slates sticking four or five feet out of the edge of the valley, a platform as Gwyn and Alison approached it, but at its base the green mountain fell sheer to the river fifteen hundred feet below.

"How super!"

"Never been before?"

"Never!"

"Not bad, is it?"

"How does the grass manage to grow?" said Alison.

"It's the sheep are the problem," said Gwyn. "Mostyn Lewis-Jones breeds them with short left legs, and Gareth Pugh breeds short right legs. There's the boundary fence between the two farms, see, right down the mountain. Mostyn's sheep eat from right to left, and Gareth's from left to right across the slope. When they reach the fence they have to walk backwards and then start again."

"Isn't it cruel to the sheep?" said Alison.

"Why?"

"When they're on level ground."

"No. They have special stilts for the short legs," said Gwyn: "called wether-go-nimbles. It's an old Welsh craft. They used to carve them in the long winter evenings, but now they're mostly made of fire-glass."

"Gosh," said Alison.

"There's a lot more to farming than people think," said Gwyn.

"Yes," said Alison. "Gwyn! What's the matter?"

Gwyn had sunk to his knees. He fell forward with his head and arms hanging down the Ravenstone and his feet drummed the turf.

"Are you ill?"

Gwyn was red in the face and shaking all over. "It's an old Welsh custom!" he gasped. "Called – called Soaking the Saxon!"

"What! Oh!" Alison hit his shoulders. "Oh! And I believed you! You – you – oh, Gwyn!"

They both hung over the Ravenstone and scattered the sheep along the mountain with their laughter.

"Don't you dare tell anyone!" said Alison. "I'd never forgive you. Oh! Stilts –!" And she collapsed again.

Gwyn rolled over and sat on the edge of the stone. "Don't worry, girl. I don't go blabbing. By, but that was a good one!"

Alison sat up.

"If it had been anybody else I'd have wanted to die," she said. "If it had happened at a party – I really did believe you! You won't tell?"

"No. It'd spoil it."

"Gosh, it's the funniest thing in years."

"You're a strange girl," said Gwyn. "One minute you're petrified, the next you haven't a care in the world. I suppose it's the same as toothache: when it stops it doesn't bother you until the next time."

"It's only – that: the owls," said Alison. "They frighten me."

"Come here, you strange girl," said Gwyn, "and listen. We've had a good laugh, and we're on top of the mountains, and it's a sunny day, and there's nothing to be frightened of. But you must listen, because we've got to go back soon."

"I can see why these valleys make good reservoirs," said Alison. "All you have to do is put a dam across the bottom end."

"Not the most tactful remark," said Gwyn. "But you're dead right."

"It's quite a thought, though," said Alison. "That thin bit of silver down there would fill the whole valley in time, and we'd be sitting here on the edge of a lake. Clive was wrong! This would be just the spot for fishing – better than his old pools, anyway."

"Have you noticed how you can hear the river, even though it's so far off? said Gwyn. "And the motorbike going up the pass? Sound rises. Listen to that river. It's what lasts. Wherever you go you can think of that noise, and you know what you hear in your head is in the valley at the same moment. It never stops. It never has stopped since it began. It was the last sound Lleu Llaw Gyffes heard before he was killed. Gronw heard it, in his turn. We hear it now."

"Gwyn—"

"Shh. Don't be frightened. Listen."

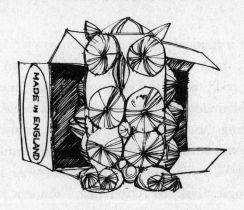

CHAPTER SEVENTEEN

"SUPPOSE," SAID GWYN. "Just suppose, a long time back, hundreds and hundreds of years, someone, somehow, did something in this valley. Suppose he found a way to control some power, or force, and used it to make a woman out of flowers. And suppose it went wrong — got out of hand — I don't know. It got out of hand because it wasn't neutral any more. There was a brain behind it. Do you follow? Neutral like a battery, I mean. You can use it to explode a bomb or to fry an egg: it depends on you."

"What is the power?" said Alison.

"I can't explain," said Gwyn. "I once saw a nettle growing in an old garage in Aber. A pale little thing it was. It had split the concrete floor."

"I wonder how he felt when he saw what he'd done," said Alison. "It'd be enough to send him off his head. But why wasn't it finished with long ago?"

"I don't think it can be finished," said Gwyn. "I think this valley really is a kind of reservoir. The house, look, smack in the middle, with the mountains all round, shutting it in, guarding the house. I think the power is always there and always will be. It builds up and builds up until it has to be let loose – like filling and emptying a dam. And it works though people. I said to Roger that I thought the plates were batteries and you were the wires."

"If the force was in the plates," said Alison, "I've let it out, and everything's right again. Oh, Gwyn, is it?"

"No. This is what frightens me. It's not as quick as that. The force was in the plates, and in the painting, but it's in us now. That's where the pattern's gone. And Huw's trying to deal with it."

"Huw? Why him?"

"He's a descendant of Gwydion, or of Lleu Llaw Gyffes: it comes to the same thing. You wouldn't credit it, but it must be true. And all his talk is something he can't quite remember, or can't quite forget. He doesn't understand it, mind: it's more of an instinct with him, it's that deep. For instance, he says the painting was done by his uncle – well, you saw how old it was, didn't you? But I bet he's not wrong. It's a question of which uncle!"

"But Huw's a labourer," said Alison.

"And what else could he be here?" said Gwyn. "He's not a labourer to the people in this valley. I'll tell you that much. It's a queer word they use for him: old, too: can't give you the English, but it's something between 'sir' and 'master' and 'father' – respectful and friendly, very clannish. Anyway, Huw's – responsible."

"Gwyn, are you sure about all this?"

"Of course I'm not sure. If I was back in Aber I'd laugh the whole thing off and say we were barmy. But I'm here in the valley, and it's an answer that fits. Give me a better one and I'll jump at it."

"You're right," said Alison. "I know you are. I've felt it, but couldn't put it into words like you can. Look at this sick valley, Gwyn. Tumbledown buildings: rough land. I saw two dead sheep on the way up the track. Even poor old Clive can't catch a tiddler. Maybe once the power's loose things'll be better, until the next time—"

"Don't talk like that, girl," said Gwyn.

"We ought to be going back," said Alison. "Thanks for telling me, Gwyn."

"You mustn't give in to it. It could burn you out."

"I'm not giving in."

"You look miserable."

"No. I've been so happy this afternoon: I can understand how she feels always alone. No wonder she's cruel. What will happen next?"

"I've no idea," said Gwyn. "We must watch out, though."

"It's going to be hard to see each other," said Alison. "My mother's dug her toes in, and she won't budge."

"This is more important than your Mam," said Gwyn. "If there is anything you're to come at once. And we'll meet each day by the seat in the kitchen garden. You can't be snooped on there, the hedge is too thick. What time?"

"About four," said Alison. "She's usually resting in the afternoons."

"No more head-in-the-sand, either," said Gwyn.

"I'll explain to Roger," said Alison. "We're all in it, aren't we?"

Gwyn stood up. "I suppose we are. I can't trust myself to leave his nose unbent, though, so you'd better tell him. Red, black and green, is it? I wonder who's the earth."

"Sorry," said Alison. "I'm not with you."

"Try changing the plug on your record player some time, if you have one: you'll see."

"It's a portable," said Alison.

"A portable?" said Gwyn. "Is it here? Will it play?"

"Yes. Why?"

"I'd like to borrow it for a few hours," said Gwyn, "if Mummy will let you. Come on, girl. Home again, home again, jiggety-jig."

They walked back to the peat road.

"You might find out some more about your father's cousin," said Gwyn.

"Bertram?"

"Yes. What happened to him? What kind of a person was he?"

"I'll try," said Alison. "Is it to do with this? There's a sort of fake mystery about him. I've noticed whenever he's mentioned Mummy goes all tragic. She doesn't actually say anything — it's the way she nods her head. I think she enjoys it."

"Well, see what you can dig up, will you?" said Gwyn.

They stopped at the scree where Gwyn had been hiding.

"You take the high road, and I'll take the low road," said Gwyn. "And I'll be insolvent afore ye— Come on, Alison, cheer up. Please don't look so miserable."

"I'm happy," said Alison. "Gwyn. I want you to do something."

Gwyn bowed.

"Wait by the hen house now," said Alison. "I'll have to be quick. But wait."

"That's easy," said Gwyn. "Well. I'd better go."

"Yes."

"Tomorrow, then. Four o'clock."

"Yes. And the hen house."

"And the hen house."

"Gwyn."

"What?"

"Don't let her: the school."

Gwyn came back up the hillside.

"She'll not wreck my chances," he said. "Shall I tell you? If I go behind that counter, there's night school. And that's not all. I've been planning. If I go behind that counter, there's nobody'll keep me there. I've been saving up, and I've bought a set of records, and if I go behind that counter I'll buy a record player. Night school's not everything. I can tell you, Alison. I couldn't anyone else. But I can tell you.

These records. They teach you to speak properly. That's what matters. That, and night school."

"No!"

"What's wrong?"

"There's nothing wrong with the way you speak, except when you're putting it on to annoy people."

"But I'm a Taff, aren't I?"

"It doesn't matter," said Alison. "I like it. It's you, and not ten thousand other people. It doesn't matter, Gwyn!"

"It doesn't matter – as long as you haven't got it!" said Gwyn, and he rattled down the scree to the water.

Alison watched him out of sight, then she walked along the peat road, off the mountain, past the barn and the sheep dip, over the ford, and climbed through the garden to the house.

Inside the house was dark and cool, and Alison heard the tea trolley in the parlour. She hurried upstairs, and a few seconds later came down again and went out through the cloakroom.

She found Gwyn sitting on the tree stump by the hen hut.

"Here," said Alison. "I want to give you a present." She pushed a box into Gwyn's hand.

"What for?"

"For today."

"I haven't anything for you, girl."

"Never mind," said Alison, and she ran back through the wood.

Gwyn opened the box. "Greetings from the Land of Song", he read. He turned the box over. "A Keltikraft Souvenir". And then the small lettering at the bottom. "Made in England".

Chapter Eighteen

"Not a sausage," said Roger, "except thirty-six frames of trees on a hill. It must have been a fluke with the other batch."

"I dare say," said Clive.

"But will you buy me some more film when you're shopping?" said Roger. "I've had enough fir trees, but there's plenty to do here – some nice composition."

"Right you are. Oops!" Clive swung at the ball and missed.

"Game set and match," said Roger.

"Phoo! It's those wide uns that catch me," said Clive. "I'm a bit long in the tooth for Ping-Pong."

"Your spinners are the dirtiest I've seen," said Roger. "The ball doesn't even bounce. How do you manage it?"

"Aha," said Clive. "Trade secret. Where's Ali? I thought

Chapter Eighteen

she was coming for a knock-up."

"Margaret took her for a walk instead."

"Oh. I see."

"Dad, when are we going home?"

"Nearly three weeks, isn't it?" said Clive.

"Any chance of going sooner?"

"Why? Aren't you enjoying it here?"

"No."

"What's up? We couldn't ask for better weather."

"It's not that."

"Don't you hit it off with Margaret and Ali? I know it's often sticky at first – these things – you know? They usually shake down all right in the end."

"That'd be the same whether we're here or not," said Roger. "It's this place that's giving me the pip. I've got to get out."

"Whoa back," said Clive. "You're kicking over the traces, that's all. Everyone goes through it. It'll pass."

"Dad, please let's go home."

"No can do," said Clive. "We're geared to stay the three weeks, and it'd be no end of a palaver if we changed."

"A lot of work for Margaret," said Roger.

"That's it," said Clive. "Hello, here's my favourite princess. Had a nice outing?"

Alison came into the table-tennis room holding a box camera by the strap.

"Yes thanks."

"Good. We've just finished a game. If you want one I'm

afraid Roger will have to hold the fort alone: I'm done for. He's had me chasing round till I'm blue in the face. I'll score, if you like."

"I hadn't come for a game," said Alison. "Roger, could you develop this film for me, please?"

"What, now?"

"Please. Before tea. Mummy and I've been taking snaps, and Mummy asked if you would, so can you see how they've turned out?"

"It's not as simple as that," said Roger. "It takes time. Won't it wait?"

"Do what you can, there's a good lad," said Clive.

"OK," said Roger. "But I know what it'll be – poor definition, bad grouping, too far away from the subject, sun on the lens, camera shake – the lot."

They walked together along the path behind the stables. Roger stopped at the end door. He put his ear to it.

"Dad."

Clive and Alison came back.

"Listen. What can you hear?"

"Somebody moving about inside?" said Clive. "Rustling."

"Any footsteps?" said Roger.

"Um – no."

"The door's padlocked, and there's no other way in," said Roger, "and I heard exactly the same thing last week."

"Did you, by Jove!" said Clive. "Let's find out what it is, then."

"None of the keys fit: I've tried."

"We'll see about that," said Clive. "Old Hoojimmaflip's at the front, raking the drive. I'll give him a shout." He went round the corner of the building. "Ahoy! Here a minute, will you?"

"What are you looking so green for?" said Roger.

"I can smell petrol," said Alison. "It makes me sick."

"Now then," said Clive. He came back with Huw Halfbacon. "This door. Let's have it open."

"No, sir," said Huw.

"It's locked. Where's the key?"

"It is not opening," said Huw. "That is a beauty padlock see."

"Yes," said Clive. "We: want: the: key."

"No, sir."

"The key, Halfbacon. Where's the key?"

"Gone, sir."

"You mean lost?"

"In the river," said Huw. "Old time. She locked the door and threw the key."

"What the blazes for?" said Clive.

"Yes, sir. Now excuse me: I must go working to Mrs Bradley."

Huw shambled away.

"No one," said Clive, "no one can be that dense! It's a conspiracy!"

"They're mad, every one of them," said Roger. "The way they smile and nod their heads, and they could be saying anything. You never know where you are with them. Please, Dad, let's pack up and go home."

"Steady on," said Clive. "I think we're being a bit imaginative. They can't all be as cuckoo as that."

"Can't they?" said Roger. "I'll tell you something. I noticed it by chance. This wasn't being done for anyone's benefit. You know I've been swimming every afternoon — well, four days ago I was walking up from the river along the farm road by the kitchen garden, and I happened to notice that Gwyn character sitting on the seat — you know, the one that's let into the very thick part of the hedge nearest the house. He was just sitting."

"What's wrong with that?" said Clive.

"The next day," said Roger, "he was there again. And since then I've been watching, and every afternoon at four o'clock he comes and sits on the seat for half an hour. He doesn't do anything. He sits, and he glowers, and then he goes. Every day! The same time! And you can see he's not enjoying himself: he's not doing it for the view. Now if he's supposed to be the bright one, what does that make the others?"

"Have you thought about the madman who jumps in the river at the same time every day, and then goes spying?" said Alison.

"Give us that film," said Roger. "Let's see what masterpieces of the art we have here." He went off, swinging the camera.

Clive sat on the edge of the fish tank and mopped his

neck. "You wouldn't believe it possible not to get a bite out of that river," he said. "Weather like this, not a breath of wind – I dunno. I'll be reduced to trawling for the beggars in this tank soon."

Alison sat by him. She kept looking at the water and then up to her bedroom.

"Odd about that door," said Clive. "I'd have sworn there was somebody inside. What's the place used for?"

"I don't know," said Alison. "I've never been in."

"It's always locked?"

"I can't remember. There are so many empty rooms."

"Odd. I don't like to feel I'm being bamboozled by domestics, and that Halfbacon fellow was definitely, but definitely, playing me up."

"His English isn't very good," said Alison.

"It's not that bad," said Clive. "Ah well. Who did he say lost the key?"

"She," said Alison.

"She who?"

"She nobody."

"Nancy?" said Clive. "I wonder. Could be. I'll ask her."

Alison dipped her hand in the water.

"Enjoying your holiday?" said Clive.

"Yes, thank you, Clive."

"Three more weeks, isn't it?"

"Yes."

"Almost."

"Oh: yes," said Alison.

"Er – how's your mother liking it?"

"Fine. Mummy adores the country – walks, and picking things up. We brought some feathers back today: lovely pale creamy ones with brown wavy bars round the edges."

"You don't want to go home early, then?" said Clive.

"Why?"

"I was thinking you might be a wee bit out of sorts with it lately. I was thinking you might not be very happy here."

"Clive, you're the kindest man I've ever met," said Alison.

"Easy does it, Mata Hari!"

They laughed.

Gwyn came up the path from the kitchen garden on to the drive. He hesitated when he saw Clive and Alison by the tank and looked over his shoulder. Then he walked away towards the yard.

Clive turned his wrist. "Twenty past four," he said. "Well I never."

Alison played with the water.

"I think I'll drift along and have a word with old Nance before tea," said Clive.

"I'll stay here," said Alison.

"Might be as well. You never know what you'll find with that lady, do you?"

When Clive had gone Alison watched her reflection in the water. At first she was trying to decide whether what she saw now was what she had seen from her bedroom, but as she held her own gaze for minute after minute it became harder for her to look away. She dared not look away, because she knew that she herself was being watched.

What is it? Something's happened. Something's stopped. Something's stopped. What? The rake!

Alison swivelled round. Huw Halfbacon was leaning on his rake, his head forward, fixed on her. Alison tried to stare him out, but in the end she had to act as if she had been thinking of something else. She turned – and looked straight into another pair of eyes: the same intense blue. It was Gwyn. He was in the dining-room window. There was no quiet in his eyes, nothing that Alison had seen when he had sat where she was now. Huw was still there. Alison felt gripped between their looking as if between pincers.

Stop peering at me.

If she moved she had either to pass Huw and go in by the front door, or to walk towards the dining-room window to reach the cloakroom.

She tossed her hair. A motorcycle engine broke into life, and its sound moved away up the road. She wrinkled her nose against the fumes.

Huw and Gwyn were still watching her, but the disturbance had loosened their grip. She could ignore them.

"Ali! Ali! Why didn't you tell me? Where did you take this?" Roger came charging out of the cloakroom, and a big sheet of wet paper was plastering itself over his arms and chest. "Quick! Here! What is it?"

"Oh, that," said Alison. "I saw there was one number left, so I snapped your Bryn thing from the road as we came past. You've been muttering about it for so long, I did it for a lark. I only pointed the camera: didn't bother with the viewfinder. It was just to use the film up."

"What's this? There. Between those two fir trees on the left."

"Why are you making such a fuss?" said Alison. "It's only Gwyn."

CHAPTER NINETEEN

HE'D A FAIR old job, throwing that spear.

Gwyn had found the Stone of Gronw, but from where he stood among the trees on the Bryn it was no different from all the other rocks. The Bryn commanded the valley, and he could watch Alison's movements and be ready for any chance, but there was no chance.

Then it was time to go to the kitchen garden. She did not come.

Tea. When he saw her laughing with her stepfather by the water Gwyn's hand squeezed the box in his pocket. She had laughed like that on the Ravenstone. He looked over his shoulder at its point on the skyline. He wanted to crush the box, to hear the shells crack, and he imagined himself crossing the lawn: he would flip the box into the water between them, discarded, litter.

Gwyn walked towards the yard.

"Where you been all afternoon?" said Nancy.

"Out," said Gwyn.

"Fine time I've had, not a hand's turn to help me," said Nancy.

"Oh, drop dead, you miserable cow."

"Is that what they teach you at the Grammar?" said Nancy.

"I wish it was," said Gwyn. " 'A' Level Profanity – by, that'd be worth taking."

"Well, right now you can take this tea trolley."

Gwyn pushed the trolley through the dining-room. From the dark of the room Alison and her stepfather, sitting together outside, were as brightly lit as if they were on stage. Gwyn watched, and when Clive left Alison he moved to the window.

Look at me, girl. Look this way. Look. Look. Look.

Alison was studying her reflection. As the minutes went by she became more and more absorbed. Gwyn lifted his hand to rap on the window, but changed his mind.

No. Your creeping Mam's somewhere. We'll do it this way. I'll show you who's boss. You'll look. You will look.

Alison started to fidget. She was no longer interested in the water.

That's it, girl…

When Gwyn returned to the kitchen his mother was not there, but he heard her walking about in the flat above, backwards and forwards, again and again, then a bump.

More walking. She was in Gwyn's room.

Gwyn went upstairs.

The old leather suitcase was on Nancy's bed, and she was flinging clothes out of drawers and cupboards.

"Come here," said Nancy. "I got a bone to pick with you, my lad."

"What are you doing?" said Gwyn.

"Clearing out," said Nancy. "I told him!"

"We're going?"

"Forty-eight hours. From tomorrow. And I don't want no references nor no in lieus. I'm off. I told him."

"Only two more days?" said Gwyn. "Only two days? Mam, not yet. Please, Mam."

"How did he find out? What you been saying behind my back?"

"Nothing, Mam."

"Nobody seen what I done with that key. Nobody. You, is it? Soft-soaping me, and then running to them with your tales?"

"No, Mam! What key?"

"After all I done for you. Running to them with your tales. Think you're one of them now, don't you? Know it all, don't you? Right, my lad. Right. You know where you're starting next month. That's you finished, boy!"

"I'll come back when you're more civilized," said Gwyn.

He managed to close the door of the flat behind him and to walk down the stairs. He was at the bottom of the stairs. He sat on the bottom step, his head in his hands, and there was nothing else he could do. Through the distance inside him he heard footsteps far away, and voices, and rustling, and through his wet fingers he saw two pairs of shoes stop in front of him, then move round him, and he felt the wood creak, and he was alone again and no one had said his name.

"How absolutely embarrassing," Roger shut the door. "It's disgusting." He laid the print on his bed.

"Haven't you ever cried?" said Alison.

Roger stretched a nylon washing line across a corner of the room and hung the print from it.

"Haven't you?" said Alison.

"Don't be an idiot," said Roger.

"You've not answered my question."

"Years ago, maybe: not recently: and certainly not in public."

"What about when your mother left?"

"Shut it!"

"Don't be coarse."

"You've heard nothing yet," said Roger.

"I only asked."

"And I'm only telling you. Shut it."

"I don't know why you're so thin-skinned about your parents," said Alison. "You've done pretty well out of it."

"Meaning what?" said Roger.

"Or your father has," said Alison. "Clive's sweet, but he's a bit of a rough diamond, isn't he? Mummy's people were very surprised when she married him."

"Yes, she was pretty damned quick off the mark, for a widow," said Roger. "Does she always home on to the nearest bank book?"

"Roger!"

Roger moved the print along the washing line. Alison sat on the bed, and twisted a thread in the counterpane.

"I ought to go and see what's the matter with Gwyn."

"On your head be it," said Roger. "But I'd leave well alone, if I were you. A couple more days and you'll have no problems."

"You're hateful."

"Now then, Ali," said Roger. "This place'll be a lot better without those two weirdies: admit. I shouldn't be surprised if the whole thing's a put-up job between them and that Halfbacon moron to scare us out so they can dig up the treasure. Or is this a smugglers' headquarters? The very nerve-centre of the illicit Welsh whisky trade!"

"You're not even vaguely funny," said Alison. "You know that what Gwyn told me makes sense, and if it was anybody else you'd agree."

"What, that battery-and-wires hogwash?"

"You feel he's right," said Alison. "I know you do. You can't bear to think he's cleverer that you are, that's your trouble. You couldn't have worked it out like Gwyn has."

"You call that working it out? That moonshine? That clap-trap? Oh, he's smart. Too smart. He'd got it all pat the day after you found those plates, hadn't he? The very next day. That's smart, all right!"

"He knows instinctively. He belongs here."

"Instinctively? Do me a favour! He wants to believe it. Him and Baconbonce – they never stop yakking. You can talk yourself into anything, if you try."

"Like now?"

"Like hell."

"You're stupid," said Alison.

"I may be stupid," said Roger. "But I'm not blubbing on the stairs."

"Perhaps you never had cause to."

"Perhaps. Ali, let's stop this. OK, he's intelligent: but he's not one of us, and he never will be. He's a yob. An intelligent yob. That's all there is to it."

"What will you do when you leave school?" said Alison.

"Go in with Dad, of course."

"What do you want to do?"

"I've told you—"

"You want to?"

"Yes. Well. What else?"

"You like photography," said Alison, "and you're good at it. Yes you are. Wouldn't you like to be a photographer?"

"I might not be good enough," said Roger.

"You don't know till you try."

"You mean professionally? What would I use for money? It takes years to become established. Anyway, Dad has it all lined up for me."

"I'm serious," said Alison. "If you wanted to be a photographer, what would Clive say?"

"He'd make the wallpaper curl."

"And what would you do? Would you stick out against him?"

"Would you against Margaret?"

"I don't know," said Alison. "It's terrible. I've never felt anything that strongly."

"I can always do it in my spare time," said Roger. "As a hobby. What's started you off on this?"

"Gwyn," said Alison. "He's upset me."

"You're not the only one he's upset!"

"What do you think'll happen to him?" said Alison. "What will he do with himself?"

"He'll be a teacher, or something equally wet."

"His mother's threatening to make him leave school and work in a shop."

"Then he'll work in a shop," said Roger.

"Can't you realize?" said Alison. "He has to find everything for himself."

"Do him a world of good."

"And the awful part is, he knows this, but he doesn't know where to begin. It's ghastly. He's — he's — oh, Roger, he's saved up and bought an elocution course on gramophone records."

"You'd never guess, to listen to him," said Roger.

"He can't use them. He hasn't got a record player. That's what I mean. Doesn't it make you feel ashamed?"

"Not really."

"You smell of petrol," said Alison.

"It was that rush job I did on your film," said Roger. "And it'll be meths, not petrol."

"It's petrol," said Alison. "I feel sick."

CHAPTER TWENTY

THE WEATHER CHANGED overnight. A wind came, dragging clouds along the mountains.

Gwyn packed. Nancy went about in silence and did her work with a perfection that made the house unbearable.

The valley was sealed by cloud.

"It's four o'clock, girl. Aren't you forgetting something?"

Alison dropped her sketch pad. Gwyn was in the parlour doorway.

"What are you doing here?"

"I'm standing next to a chaise longue."

"You're not allowed in here," said Alison.

"Sorry, Miss. Will I get the sack?"

"Mummy may come!"

"What's that to me?" said Gwyn. "I'm going the day after tomorrow. Alison – tomorrow: one day. Where've you been, girl?"

"Mummy saw us up the mountain. She was watching through binoculars. She was waiting for me – and now I daren't. I just daren't. Gwyn, please go."

"I'm going after tomorrow, first thing. So I'm here now. I've nothing to lose."

"But I have!" said Alison. "You don't know!"

"You'd better tell me, then," said Gwyn. "I'm listening."

"Go away—"

"Neat fireplace, isn't it?" said Gwyn. "Those tiles hand-painted, are they?"

Alison knocked open the catch on the french window and ran from the house on to the drive.

"The kitchen garden's over there," said Gwyn. He had caught up with her in a few strides.

"Go away!" said Alison. "Anyone can see us!"

"Not likely," said Gwyn. "But the kitchen garden's nice and quiet. Or shall we stay here? Your wish is my command."

The kitchen garden was at the end of a path below the drive. It was shut off from the rest of the grounds by a slate wall and a hedge. The gate pierced the hedge, which was high, and thick and deep. A seat made from old ship's timbers was set in the hedge for the view out over the river to the mountains.

"That ravine up there is where the foxes go," said Gwyn. "The Black Hiding. They go up the waterfalls, see, and the cliffs are that steep nothing can come at them, and the hounds lose the scent, and they lie till it's safe. Then they skip out at the top in the peat. Cunning."

"What do you want?" said Alison.

"You asked me that before," said Gwyn. "The answer's not changed. You have."

"No, Gwyn. You don't understand. I daren't see you. Mummy's threatened what she'll do, and she means it."

"And what's that?" said Gwyn. "What can she do? Hang you in chains in the family dungeon? Lock you in a turret? Your name Rapunzel or something, is it? What can she do, girl? Shoot you?"

"You don't understand—"

"I don't understand. I understand what it's been like since we went up the mountain: I'll give you that free, girl. Your Mam couldn't do anything worse than these last five days. Go on, you tell me."

"Mummy says – if I talk to you again – she'll make me – I'll have to – she says I'll have to leave the choir."

"What?" said Gwyn.

"She means it. I'll have to leave the choir. And she won't renew my subscription."

"Subscription," said Gwyn.

"For the tennis club."

"Club."

"You see, Gwyn—"

"See! See! See! See!" Gwyn flung his head back against the wood. "See! See!"

"Don't make that noise! Everyone'll hear!"

"You think I care?" said Gwyn. "She said that, did she, your Mam?"

"Yes."

"And you didn't tell her what she could do with the choir and the tennis?"

"What do you mean?"

"That's why you've not come these last five days."

"I wouldn't play tricks on you, Gwyn. I simply daren't come."

"It did happen," said Gwyn. "We were up there on the mountain. It did all happen."

"Of course," said Alison. "It was lovely."

"And you gave me a box," said Gwyn. He put his hand in his mackintosh pocket. "This box. Why?"

"I was happy. I wanted to give you a present," said Alison.

"And the choir and the tennis," said Gwyn. "You put that against – this."

"It's Mummy. I can't bear to see her hurt or upset."

"No," said Gwyn. "No. All right, girl."

"Don't be angry," said Alison. "You frighten me when you're angry."

"I'm not angry," said Gwyn. "Never mind. Did you find out about your cousin?"

"Yes," said Alison. "He was very clever with his hands. All those animals in the billiard-room are his work, and he made the cases for them."

"What else?"

"That's all. Mummy wouldn't tell me any more."

"Nothing about how he was killed?"

Alison shook her head.

"Shall I tell you, then?" said Gwyn.

"You know?" said Alison. "How did you manage that?"

"In for a penny in for a pound," said Gwyn. "I thought my Mam would have an idea about what's going on, so I whipped some of your stepfather's fags for her as bait. She only nibbled, though: but she did mention this Bertram. Then a couple of nights back I siphoned off half a glass of port from the decanter – it's all she needs – and she was in the right mood to get a kick out of pinching it. And that was that. By!"

"What?"

"Well, she as good as said Huw did him in, but I shouldn't worry. No, cousin Bertram snuffed it up the pass there: road accident."

"Is that all?" said Alison. "The way Mummy's always rolled her eyes I thought he must have killed himself, at least. I used to make up stories about him: he was crossed in love: she'd Married Another. He looked that sort in his photographs. Very dashing."

"Bit too dashing," said Gwyn. "You were right about good with his hands. He had this vintage motorbike, see. Done it up himself. Then one day he's coming over the pass – one-in-four just there – and he failed to negotiate a bend, as they say. He'd left his brakes at home. The bike jammed itself on some slate, but he went three hundred feet – kerchoom, kerchoom, aaaaargh, splat! – Alison!"

Alison screwed up her eyes and her mouth was drawn tight.

"I'm a fool," said Gwyn. "I didn't mean to upset you. I didn't know you cared about him. You said you'd never seen him. Alison!"

She straightened up. "It's not that," she said. "Sorry. I'm all right. Something else. Gwyn, I must go. I must go. It's tea time."

"You look ill," said Gwyn.

"I'll be fine in a minute."

"You'll come tomorrow," said Gwyn.

"I can't."

"There's only tomorrow."

"I daren't."

"I'm going back to Aber."

"I know."

"Tomorrow, Alison. Please. Can't you see? You must."

"Stop it," said Alison. "Stop it, stop it! Stop tearing me between you. You and Mummy! You go on till I don't know who I am, what I'm doing. Of course I can see! Now. But afterwards she starts, and what she says is right, then."

"I only want you to be yourself," said Gwyn.

"And what's that?" said Alison. "What you make me? I'm one person with Mummy, and another with you. I can't argue: you twist everything I say round to what you want. Is that fair?"

"You will be here, won't you?" said Gwyn. "Tomorrow. It's the last time."

Chapter Twenty

"Gwyn."

"Please."

"How now, brown cow?" Roger called. "Are you having trouble, Ali?"

He was climbing through the hedge at the other side of the garden.

"What's he on about?" said Gwyn.

"Nothing," said Alison.

"What's that brown cow?"

"Nothing, Gwyn."

"Tea, Ali," said Roger.

"Yes: I'm coming."

"How's the rain in Spain?" said Roger. "Still mainly on the plain?"

"What's he on about, Alison?"

"I say, that's a smart mackintosh you're wearing," said Roger. "Those trend-setting short sleeves, and up-to-the-minute peep-toe plimsolls—"

"Be quiet, Roger," said Alison.

"What's that about cows and rain?" said Gwyn.

"Don't tell me you haven't reached the lesson yet," said Roger. "Surely it comes on the very first record."

"Roger!"

"You told him?" whispered Gwyn. "You told him? Told him?"

"No!" said Alison.

"You told him. Was it a good laugh?"

"No, Gwyn!"

"I bet it was. What else? What else was funny?"

"You're wrong!"

"You won't have told him about the stilts, will you? Not when you'd got the big laugh."

"Not that way, Gwyn! I promise it wasn't!"

"Couldn't run back quick enough, could you?" said Gwyn.

"You're not quite on the ball, actually," said Roger. "Ali didn't say much. I mean, I don't know whether you're using the complete Improva-Prole set, or the shorter course of Oiks' Exercises for getting by in the Shop. She didn't say really."

"Alison." Gwyn backed from them. "Alison."

"Gwyn! Don't look at me like that. Don't."

"Alison."

"Don't! Don't look at me like that! – Don't! – I can't stand it!"

"Alison."

"Don't – Don't look at me! – Don't! – Stop him, Roger! Roger, make him stop. Make him! Make him! Make him!"

"Now, Ali, it's OK. It's OK. Calm down. It's all right, Ali. He's done a bunk. He's gone. I told you he was a yob."

CHAPTER TWENTY-ONE

HIS FACE WAS in wet grass. He tore at his breath, sprawled among bracken and a knee hard against slate, but no pain. He looked through the bend of his elbow and saw the house a long way off. The cloud line was only yards above him, like smoke. He had no memory of reaching the mountain.

He lay till he could move, then walked up towards the grey air of the mountain. He would be safe outside the valley, he would make plans, where to go, how to eat, to sleep.

The cloud drifted with him, always in front, blocking his sight, and the mountain was open below him down to the house, but he could not look. He set his back to the valley, thrusting left right left right, a foot of mountain and a second of time behind him, and so for a while nothing else mattered.

He rested when he knew the house had gone. Most of the valley was hidden from where he leant against a quartz boulder under the edge of the plateau. He held a clover to strip the petals, and reached for another, and it was then that he saw how it grew in a white line of flowers past the boulder and into the cloud.

He crouched by a flower, but his hand drew back, for the grass round the clover had been flattened, though the clover stood free. As he watched, a blade sprang, and slowed, lifting its weight.

He went downhill a few paces. His feet had crushed grass and flower, but where he had not trodden yet the clover stood above the grass.

More blades sprang back, as if they had been flattened by a light step.

Somebody up there, is it?

He walked beside the white track and the cloud moved in front of him like skirts until he was on the plateau. The ground was level. There was no more climbing, and the mist lifted from the mountain and he saw across peat and water and rushes, and there was no one on the mountain but himself. In the distance a black sow rubbed its flank against the cairn.

Gareth Pugh's.

Now then. Which road?

Which?

He saw mountains wherever he looked: nothing but mountains away and away and away, their tops hidden sometimes, but mountains with mountains behind them in desolation for ever. There was nowhere in the world to go.

"Alison—"

He stood, and the wind was cold through him. He looked again, but there was nothing, and the sky dropped lower, hiding the barren distances, crowding the hills with ghosts, then lifting, and he looked again. Nothing. Even the pig had gone.

He stumbled along the mountain. I'll show them. You could die here, man, and who'd care? Them?

He had not meant to find the Ravenstone. He came to it when he could see no more than three paces ahead. He faced the wind, ready for the cloud to pass, and there were the valley and the house. For a moment he longed to be among fields and trees, with people, to be down from the moss and the peat hags.

But the sheep were moving from left to right across the slopes. Wether-go-nimbles. He raged the cold back into him.

Farmers whistled their dogs, and called. The sounds rose from the valley, "There, Ben. There, Ben. Good, Ben," and he saw the dogs fanning through the bracken, black and white among the green. "There, Ben. Lass. Good, Lass. There. There. There." The dogs changed direction at a whistle. He looked for the men, but they were not on the mountain. "Bob, there, Bob, Lass, good, Lass, there."

The dogs came on and the sheep bunched together. The dogs were in a bent line, the horns of the line pointing up the mountain. The dogs reached the sheep. "There there there there. Ben. There. Bob, Bob, Bob." The whistles followed sharp and urgent. The dogs swept past the sheep, ignored them, the horns of the line drew in, pointed to the Ravenstone.

"There, Ben. There, Ben. Good, Lass."

He looked behind him. There were no sheep on the top.

"Bob, stay, Bob. There, Ben, there, Ben. Lass, there. Lass."

The dogs came for the Ravenstone. Their tongues rolled with the climb, but they came, and when they were near they dropped their bellies low, and crept. They moved in short spurts, eyes fixed.

He could not watch all of them at the same time.

They moved past the Ravenstone, turned, and lay between their haunches, and then ran at him, low quick darts from all sides. When he faced a dog it stopped, and two others closed nearer, and lay still when he looked, and the first came on.

"Get out!"

He waved his arms.

"Ben. Good, Ben. There, Ben."

A wall-eyed dog had reached him first, in with a nip to the ankle and away. He ran to kick it, but other teeth pinched his calf.

"Lass, Lass, Lass, there, Lass."

"Call your flaming dogs off!"

But his voice went into cloud, and the wind spread it over the peat moss.

Two dogs rushed him, and he fell from the Ravenstone on to the steep grass and slid for twenty yards, sky, teeth, mountain and tongues whirling, and then he was on his feet and his own weight carried him down, and the whistling grew louder, but the dogs were silent – rush, stop, belly to the ground, rush, nip and away.

"Good, Ben. Good, Lass. Ben, there, Ben. Good, Bob."

From the grass to the screes and the bracken, and grass again, over the streams they drove him. If he threw stones at them they snarled and were more savage in their biting. He ran, fell, ran a thousand feet down to the river, but they would not leave him. No men appeared, but the shouts and whistles were close in the hedgebanks. The dogs walked up the road, their steps high and slow, lips arched red, back, back, to the front drive – and left him. They cocked their legs at the gatepost, and frisked into the meadow.

"Good, Ben. Good, Lass. Good, Bob. Here. Here. Here. Good, Ben."

Who told them? Who told them I was going? Who said? Who knew?

He wanted to sleep. Suddenly all he wanted was to sleep.

Sleep: food: eat. Who knew I wasn't coming back? They'll not have me. What are they wanting? They didn't send dogs – before – when we – I – up: before. Who told them? Who?

Chapter Twenty-Two

"THERE YOU ARE," said Clive. "Been looking for you both."

"Hang on, Dad," said Roger. He pulled back his elbow and splayed his fingers over the green cloth. As he thrust the cue forward Alison said, "Hello, Clive."

The cue glanced off the billiard ball.

"You did that deliberately," said Roger. "Broke my concentration."

"She didn't," said Clive. "The bad workman always blames his tools. It's a cue, not a see-saw. Watch me. The cue moves easily: backwards: and forwards: one: two: one, two: level: don't lift the butt: and—"

He played five cannons in a row, and then potted the red.

"Clive, you're brilliant," said Alison.

"Evidence of a misspent youth, that's what they say."

"Why were you looking for us?" said Roger.

"Um – yes," said Clive. "Tread a bit softly these next couple of days, there's good people."

"What are we supposed to have done?" said Roger.

"I'm not bothered. But until her majesty abdicates things are a bit dicey."

"What happened?" said Alison.

"Nothing. She's playing it strictly by the book, that's all."

"I don't understand," said Alison.

"Old Nancy's complained to Margaret about the kitchen being her stamping ground until she's worked her notice. So no safaris, eh?"

"Dad, are you all right?"

"She says the larder's been cleaned out of bread and cheese."

"It wasn't me," said Roger.

"Nor me," said Alison.

"I'm not worried," said Clive. "We stock up again tomorrow. Let's weather the next couple of days, though, shall we?"

"No," said Roger. "We'll have it straight."

"Honest, Clive," said Alison.

"Oh? Well, not to worry."

"It'll be that light-fingered so-and-so she carts round with her," said Roger.

"It will be Gwyn," said Alison. "I know he does – take things."

"Does he?" said Roger. "Wait a minute, then. Have you borrowed my anorak?"

"No," said Alison.

"I saw it wasn't in the cloakroom when we came through. If he's had it I'll kick his teeth in."

"Leave it," said Clive. "We'll be rid the day after tomorrow. It's not worth making a fuss. Are you coming for dinner?"

"Yes. There's something else I bet he's found," said Roger, and on their way through the cloakroom he lifted the lid of an ammunition box by the log basket. "He has, too! Dad! He's pinched my climbing boots!"

"I'll have a word with him tonight," said Clive.

"I'll have more than a word," said Roger.

"I'd steer clear. Not worth the fuss."

"In case someone's upset?" said Roger. "She'll just have to be upset. No doubt we'll survive."

"Now watch it," said Clive.

"Once bitten twice shy, that's your motto, isn't it, Dad?"

"Right," said Clive. "Upstairs. If you decide you're fit to take dinner with the rest of us kindly see that you're ready by the gong. It's a civilized meal. We shan't expect any snotty-nosed kids who haven't learnt their manners."

"Naturally, Father," said Roger. "Good night."

"Sorry about that," said Clive. "He'll apologize."

"It doesn't matter, Clive," said Alison.

"Now look, princess. I'm the one to say whether it matters or not. Let's get that straight, shall we?"

"Excuse me."

Huw Halfbacon knocked on the open door.

Chapter Twenty-Two

"Yes, what is it?"

"Excuse me asking," said Huw. "Is the boy here?"

"Which boy? Young Gwyn?"

"That is right, sir."

"I expect so."

"We were fetching him down this afternoon, and I was wondering if he is here now."

"I think he may have gone for a walk," said Alison.

"Oh. Yes?"

"He's borrowed some climbing boots."

"Ah," said Huw.

"Last time I saw him," said Clive, "he was having a kip along the front drive there after tea. I thought he was ill at first, but he was snoring away — spark out."

"Yes, sir."

"While you're here," said Clive. "I don't suppose you can find us another housekeeper, can you?"

"Is she not good?" said Huw. "I am sorry for that."

"She's given notice. Didn't she tell you? They're off the day after tomorrow."

"She is not talking to me," said Huw.

"But is there anyone else, Halfbacon?"

"No, sir. Now excuse me. I must go working."

"Work?" said Clive. "At this time? Don't you ever knock off?"

"Yes, sir. Excuse me, when is she going, that day?"

"After breakfast."

"After breakfast," said Huw. "Well, well, sir."

"Look here, Halfbacon," said Clive. "You must understand this overtime lark is entirely your own affair. If you think you can twist my arm with it for more wages you've come to the wrong shop."

"No, sir," said Huw. He walked away. "No, no, not at all. I must go helping my uncle with finish a job, see. Good night, sir. Good night, my lady."

"Urrh," said Clive. "These people give me the jim-jams. It's the same in business. You never know where you are with them, you never have a straight answer. You never know when they're being polite or just sarky."

"Cold," said Alison.

"Eh? What?"

"Cold – kippers."

CHAPTER TWENTY-THREE

HE SAT BEHIND a thorn bush high in the valley, waiting for dusk. The first part of the climb into the rocks might be seen from the farms. He ate a little of the cheese and scooped the stream water into his hands. He was wearing both his shirts, his pullover on top of them, and the anorak, and two pairs of trousers were tucked into his socks.

These boots are a bit of all right.

He had kept low along the stream, and quiet, and he had seen no dogs, no voices had called, and no one had whistled. So far it had been easy, but now he had to climb the Black Hiding, and the noise of its waters pounded him.

It was dark enough to move. There had been hardly any rain for several weeks, and the channels were running slack, so that he could climb between the loose slate of the cliffs and the foam of the water.

Them cliffs and screes – by, foxes know what they're at.

He climbed the narrow thread of rock, smoothed, hollowed by waterfalls. On either side the decayed buttresses of the Black Hiding rose above him and fell below him.

He rested on a flat stone, his feet hanging over the drop. Lamps were showing in the house.

Cosy is it for you down there? You can't touch me. I've done with you lot.

He ate some food, and climbed again. The top of the Black Hiding started to show, a notch against the skyline, and then it disappeared as he came in close to the stream below a waterfall: twenty feet, and no way up unless he moved out on to the crag. The buttresses crowded the water.

So how do foxes manage?

The buttress was not sheer, and he saw that an animal could take it at a run. The surface would hold long enough.

But you're not a fox, man.

He ran at the shale, and the force of his scrabbling carried him more than half way. Then he stuck. He was spread-eagled on the buttress. His toes dug into the muck and his fingers clutched deep. His head was twisted to the side. He looked down out of the corner of one eye.

Two hundred feet? What's the chances? Slide? Like a cowing cheese-grater.

His hands pulled balls of clay out of the surface, and the boots were moving farther apart.

The lamps twinkled at him from the valley.

He dragged his head up. The slab of the waterfall was less than twice his own height above him, but he was at full stretch, with nothing to thrust against.

What you worrying for? Ten seconds and you'll be on that ledge, or you won't. Them holds will go, or they won't. What's your problem? Nothing to it, man! One. Two. Three. Hup!

He spat from the slab to the crest of the waterfall. Where his hands and feet had touched there were no holds, only streaks in the shale.

He stood on the edge and rolled stones to see how he would have fallen from the buttress, then he threw stones at the house. It was nearly a mile away, but before they dropped into the crags the stones arched high and seemed as if they would reach.

Surprising what you can do when you try: as if I cared.

He turned from the valley, and climbed. He was near the top of the Black Hiding, and the water lost its fierceness, and soon he would come to the peat hags, and from there he would find the rocks that marked where some women had died in a snowstorm, and then he would be near the line of slates, upended in the moss, that pointed over the mountain to the next valley. From that valley he could reach a main road, thumb a lift, and be in Aberystwyth next morning.

The top of the Black Hiding was a deep stone gutter which ran into the plateau. Behind him the crags fell to the valley and the spark of lamplight, and over his head the grass caps of the buttresses held the last of the day.

Them cliffs and screes – by, foxes know what they're at.

He climbed the narrow thread of rock, smoothed, hollowed by waterfalls. On either side the decayed buttresses of the Black Hiding rose above him and fell below him.

He rested on a flat stone, his feet hanging over the drop. Lamps were showing in the house.

Cosy is it for you down there? You can't touch me. I've done with you lot.

He ate some food, and climbed again. The top of the Black Hiding started to show, a notch against the skyline, and then it disappeared as he came in close to the stream below a waterfall: twenty feet, and no way up unless he moved out on to the crag. The buttresses crowded the water.

So how do foxes manage?

The buttress was not sheer, and he saw that an animal could take it at a run. The surface would hold long enough.

But you're not a fox, man.

He ran at the shale, and the force of his scrabbling carried him more than half way. Then he stuck. He was spread-eagled on the buttress. His toes dug into the muck and his fingers clutched deep. His head was twisted to the side. He looked down out of the corner of one eye.

Two hundred feet? What's the chances? Slide? Like a cowing cheese-grater.

His hands pulled balls of clay out of the surface, and the boots were moving farther apart.

The lamps twinkled at him from the valley.

seven: main road by ten. Blast Gareth Pugh. Never mind, should be clear of Aber before she can get back, even if she twigs.

He ate some more food, and arranged himself on the tree. He found a compass and a whistle tied to a lanyard in the anorak pocket. He took the lanyard and made a sling round a branch, and pushed his arm through to the shoulder. Then he wedged himself between the trunk and a tangle of branches.

It was a warm night, and he was sheltered from the wind, but he could not sleep for more than a few minutes at a time. He was cold and cramped. He had no watch, but the position of the moon told him how short each sleep had been.

The lamps went out in the valley.

He dozed, and shivered, and dozed, and ate the last of the food, and dozed.

He woke. He was cold to the bone, and his head had fallen backwards across a branch, so that when he opened his eyes he was looking at the edge of the plateau thirty feet above him. The lanyard had deadened his arm, and his other arm lay over his chest, the fingers hooked in the sling. His neck was stiff. There was a man on the plateau.

The man walked along the top of the gutter towards the peat hags.

Them with their dogs, is it? There'll be a right sort-out if they tread on that pig. Let them get on with it. I'm not bothered.

He found a new position in the branches to ease his

arm. Darkness came and went with clouds over the moon, and the water rattled the stones, but he watched.

He saw the scree move before he heard any change in the note of the stream: a long slew of rubble farther up the gutter hit the water where it lay in a hollow. The bubbles rose like silver blossom.

The sheep track in the wall of the gutter touched the scree there, followed a bend in the stream, and crossed over the roots below him. He watched the track at the bend.

Sheep? That old pig?

But there was a new sound, very close, broken by the water, but he could hear it, and it went on and on – a voice, humming, mumbling, scarcely words, but it was a kind of song.

He moved his head to peer through the branches. The man was sitting at the foot of the tree.

Cripes! Now what?

The man came to the end of his song, but he did not go. He sat, swinging his legs above the stream, and pushed his cap back on his head.

"Lovely night, isn't it?"

He wiped his nose on his forearm.

"Lovely night," he said again. "Yes. Lovely. For the time of year."

CHAPTER TWENTY-FOUR

"IT IS INDEED a lovely night," said Huw.

"Leave me alone."

"You come down now, boy."

"I'm fine here."

"You're needed."

"No one needs me, and I need nothing."

"Then you are very lucky," said Huw. "What will you do with all your riches?"

"I'm clearing out. This time tomorrow I'll be in Birmingham, and that's the last you'll see of me."

"You are needed back at the house. It is nearly time."

"Leave me alone. I've had enough. Spooks or whatever it's all yours."

"You won't run away," said Huw. "You care too much."

"I don't care about anything. I nearly fell off that cliff,

and I trod on Gareth Pugh's sow, and I wasn't bothered. That's how much I care. And you want to watch out for that sow: she's a nasty pair of chompers."

"She was only stopping you from leaving the valley," said Huw.

"Not half she wasn't."

"It is always the Black Hiding," said Huw, "but you went in the wrong direction this afternoon, and we had to use the dogs to fetch you away."

"Tell me another."

"I shall tell you one other," said Huw, "then you will come down. I'm tired of your childishness."

"Thanks!"

"Not at all," said Huw. "Are you thinking yet how I came straight to you?"

"No."

"We come here," said Huw. "It is the place."

"I came here to miss the dogs, and I'm in this tree because I don't want to tread on any more pigs in the dark. If you want to make something of it that's your business."

Huw crossed the stream and pulled himself on to a ledge in the opposite wall of the gutter. "Now," he said. "You're safe. You can run back up the tree if I move, little boy. Come down and I'll show you the chance in this. Down to the foot of the tree. There. Reach into the crack where the root grows. You must put your arm right in."

"It's a dead end."

"Feel to one side," said Huw. "Careful. Careful. Take out

your hand. – Well?"

"Mister Huw: I'm sorry," said Gwyn.

He was holding a spear head in the palm of his hand. It was made of flint, and was so thin that the moon shone through it, and the fretting of its surface made it a leaf of sculpted light and stone.

"This was the spear," said Gwyn.

"A year he took to make it," said Huw. "Gronw Pebyr, Lord of Penllyn."

"It's older than that," said Gwyn. "It's very old."

"It was a long time ago," said Huw.

Gwyn put his arm back in the rock. There was a hollow at right angles to the crack at the far end, and there were several things lying inside. Most of what he touched fell to pieces before he could pull it out: leather, wood, or cloth all rotted in the wet.

He laid a stone beside the flint. It was a ball of quartz the size of his fist and a face was painted on it. It was only a simple double arch of brow, like a pick head, running to a short nose or beak, and two dots for eyes. He found this pattern again and again on all the solid things, on jars, and pebbles and a slate disc pierced to be worn on a cord round the neck. The simple line stared out, human or bird face: it was impossible to tell.

"How long has this been happening?" said Gwyn. He held the rusted fragments of a dagger in its sheath.

"There's no saying. But we of the blood must meet it in our time, and we bring here what we have."

"I didn't understand," said Gwyn. "I'm all numb inside."

"I know," said Huw.

"I felt I could blow that house up just by looking at it."

"Perhaps you could," said Huw. "Here: in this valley: now. That is how the power is spent. Through us, within us, the three who suffer every time."

"But why, Huw?"

"Because we gave this power a thinking mind. We must bear that mind, leash it, yet set it free, through us, in us, so that no one else may suffer."

"What's going to happen?"

"I don't know. She is here, the lady, and you have made her owls: she will go hunting. But don't let her destroy. She will be the worse for my fault, and my uncle's fault and my grandfather's fault, who tried to stop what can't be stopped – him with the painting, him with the plates. We built the dyke of sand, and won a little space."

"So we're in this mess because you ducked it."

"Yes."

"How?"

"Oh, it is a story, and we have suffered for it no less that if we had faced our time."

"Who's 'we'?" said Gwyn.

"Me, your mother, him."

"My Mam?"

Huw smiled. "You did not know her. She was young and lovely. There was not a girl like Nancy."

"What! Her!"

Chapter Twenty-Four

"So much harm done through so much weakness," said Huw. "You must be strong."

"But my Mam!"

"She was the winds of April."

Gwyn started to put things back into the rock.

"Huw – can I take any?"

"Have you some to leave?"

"—Yes."

"At this time, all this is yours."

Gwyn lifted the thin slate with the eye pattern on it. He took a cardboard box from the anorak pocket and tipped the shell owl on to his hand. As he stretched to place the owl next to the flint spear head in the rock "Greetings from the Land of Song" shimmered briefly in luminous paint at arm's length before he pushed it round the corner.

Gwyn put the slate in the box.

"Will you give this to Alison tomorrow?"

"You give it, boy."

"I can't. Please, Huw."

"Go on, it's better from you."

"No. Tell her it's from me."

"You give it her."

"I can't. It's no good. I can't, Huw."

"Just give it her? Is that all?"

"Say it's from me."

Gwyn hid the last pieces. He felt at the back of the hollow. "Here. There's something else. You've a long reach: let's have it."

"It's not my time to be looking there," said Huw.

"Come on, man."

"No, no, I'll not touch it."

"Never mind. I think I can – got them!"

Gwyn uncurled his first and held it to the moon.

"What are these? Pieces of – what? – rubber? What are they doing here? Rubber? That's not old. They're like sort of – brake blocks? Huw! Are these yours? Man, you did it? You knocked off Bertram?"

"Keep them away! Keep them away! He is the dark raven of my unreason! Keep them away!"

"Mam said—"

"I didn't mean it," said Huw. "He never had that old bike outside the grounds, up and down, front drive to back, that's all he ever did. Then he rode to make me jump when I was working on the drive, and he had my Nancy, and I thought I'd show him what it is to land in the rhododendrons, so I took out the blocks. He never said he was going up the pass. I didn't know! But I should have known. We could not escape, though I pebble-dashed her in the billiard-room, and hid her in the loft, and even he, the poor man, did what he thought best."

"What was that?"

"He shot her."

"Shot her? How could he? You're as mad as they said!"

Huw came down to Gwyn and held his arm.

"A lord must look to his people. I failed them in my time, and we were destroyed no less. You must not fail now.

She is terrible in her loneliness and her pain. You are lord in blood to this valley now."

"Are you sure, man?" said Gwyn. "It's a pretty bad joke from where I'm standing."

"No, no," said Huw, and his eyes searched Gwyn's face. "You are the heir."

"Heir? That's a good word, that is!" said Gwyn. "Heir to what? Don't tell me! Here's all I'll ever see of my father! I'm an heir right enough – heir to a couple of brake blocks!"

"No, no, boy, you are wrong. You are the lord in blood to this valley after me. There is not one doubt of it. I am your father. You did not know?"

Gwyn shook his head. "She never told me, Huw. She never. And she did that to you? She did that?"

"It was my ending," said Huw.

CHAPTER TWENTY-FIVE

THE RAIN FELL straight, without wind, but inside the house it could not be heard except on the kitchen skylight.

"Mustn't grumble, I suppose," said Clive. "We've had a fair crack. I'd stay in bed this morning: you're not missing much."

"I really am better," said Alison. "Mummy's a fusser. I'll get up when you've gone."

"That was a nasty temperature you started last night," said Clive. "Don't overdo things."

"I shan't, but I'll make you both a super table decoration for dinner this evening."

"Bless you," said Clive. "Cheers, then."

He went downstairs. Roger was sitting on the ammunition box in the cloakroom and prising mud from his boots with a screwdriver.

"Wet through," said Roger. "He's not even had the

decency to clean them. And look at my anorak. Plastered. What's he been at?"

"I'll fix it," said Clive, "if you'll give me the sizes."

"You've no need to buy a new lot, unless it makes you feel better," said Roger.

Clive shrugged himself into his stormcoat. "Nark it. You know we don't carry squabbles over to the next day. Clean slate each morning, right?"

"You're the boss," said Roger. "How's Ali?"

"In great form," said Clive. "It must have been one of those sudden chills. She'll be up as soon as – um."

"—The coast's clear?" said Roger.

"You wait," said Clive. "You'll find out. Women can be the very devil."

"Ah well," said Roger. "I wouldn't know, would I? I can't judge."

"No, you can't."

"That's all right, then."

"Now what's the matter?" said Clive.

"Nothing, Dad. You see to your shopping."

"I did my best," said Clive. "You can't ask for more than that. I hope you'll understand—"

"When I'm old enough," said Roger.

Clive sat on the box. "What's up?"

"Nothing, Dad."

"Growing pains?"

"For Pete's sake!" Roger threw the boots across the cloakroom.

"It's a phase we all go through," said Clive.

"I'm sorry, Dad. This house: I feel I could put a bomb under it."

"Why not come with us, and have a day out?"

"No thanks. I can't stand trailing round those shops, either."

"Can't say I blame you. But look, if it's as bad as that we'll go home. I wanted us to have a holiday, not a ruddy breakdown."

"Perhaps it's the weather," said Roger.

"Could be, could be. These hills get a bit on top of you, don't they? Well, if you're not coming I'd better be off, or it'll be midnight before we're back."

"Yes, Dad."

Roger finished cleaning the boots and stuffed them with paper, then he sat for a while, letting the screwdriver swing between his knuckles against the box. The movement slowed, stopped. "Of course," he said.

He put on his anorak, fastened the hood, and went out of the cloakroom to the back of the stables. The rain hammered on the roof, and he could hear nothing through the door when he listened.

Roger fitted the screwdriver to the head of one of the screws and leant on it. The slot gave and white metal shone in the rust, but the thread moved, and one screw followed another, and the hasp dangled from the padlock free of the door.

A mat of cobwebs filtered the light and the room was

preserved in dust, and at first Roger saw only as much as he had seen from the ladder, but when he was used to the dark he laughed.

"The old fraud!"

He ran back to the house, head down, dodging puddles. He stamped and brushed the water off in the cloakroom before he went to the bottom of the stairs.

"Ali!"

"Yes?"

"The game's up, you old fraud! Holding out on me! Come on down and explain yourself!"

"I'm washing my hair."

"Stow it, Ali! Come and tell uncle Roger about the fun and games!"

"I wish you'd talk sense, Roger."

"You've been outwitted by a mastermind, that's what. A padlock's no stronger than the screws on the hasp."

"What are you talking about?"

"Quit stalling, and hurry up! I want to know how it works."

"How what works?"

"Hurry up, Ali! I'll see you there."

"Where? Roger! Where? I don't know what you're talking about!"

"And Bubo Bubo Bubo to you!" shouted Roger.

"What?"

"With knobs on!"

Roger dived back into the rain.

Why didn't I think of it? Sneaking off so she wouldn't have to let anyone else take turns. What a fantastic job! Seems OK: a bit knocked about. Must be donkey's years old: ought to be in a museum: more a scooter than a bike.

The motorcycle was propped in a corner. The petrol tank, a tin bottle, rested on a platform behind the saddle. The wheels were small, and the handlebars were like those of an ordinary bicycle, with cable brakes, and when Roger squeezed there was no tension.

I see. Blocks missing. Now what's this other nonsense she's rigged up? An owl's tea party?

In the middle of the room stood a glass fronted case, facing the door and three feet high, and inside the case was a stuffed owl. It was a huge bird, and its yellow eyes were browed with long ear tufts like horns. There was a faded hand-written label on the glass which said: Eagle Owl (Bubo Bubo Bubo) The Bryn Ghost: laid by Eley-Kynoch Grand Prix 12 bore at 60 feet.

The girl's a nutter.

Alison's paper owls were ranged about the case, their stylized heads intent, as if they were an audience for the eagle owl.

Wait a minute. – Who was in here yesterday? Ali was with us when we heard that noise.

Roger squatted to look more closely at the owls. Each owl had made a mark with its tail in the dust, and these marks could be followed as lines along the floor, and the lines curved and wove a pattern, and it was a pattern that had the balance and precision of iron filings in the field of a magnet or of petals in a flower, and the magnet or the heart of the flower, from which all lines started and to which all lines came, was the eagle owl in its glass case.

Roger looked at the motorcycle. It was smeared clean where he had touched it, and the floor showed where he had stood, and walked, and all the rest was the unbroken dust of years, except for owl tracks.

The room was darkened from behind him. "Careful, Ali," said Roger. "I've been stupid. There's something up. I'm sorry. I hadn't seen properly. I thought you'd done it. Clear out. Quick."

The anorak muffled his head, and he had to turn his whole body to see her. From his squatting position he heard nothing, and the light showed that she was still in the doorway.

"Ali. Shift. – Ali?"

He moved round on his hands. The doorway was blocked by a figure hooded and draped in oilskins. Roger jumped back. It was Nancy. She stood there, a groundsheet slung over her, holding a poker in her hand, and her eyes were as grey as the dust.

"What do you want?" said Roger.

She did not answer.

"Haven't you any jobs?" said Roger.

Nancy ran forward and swung the poker at the case. The glass exploded, and the eagle owl flew up as a cloud of sawdust and feathers, and Nancy lashed about her at the paper models which winged in the air around the leaping woman and the dead bird that filled the room and stuck to her wet clothing and even to her skin and to her hair.

Roger huddled against the motorcycle, his arms crossed over his head to keep off the blows, but Nancy was fighting the swirled dust. She said nothing. The sounds in the room were her breathing, the whip of the poker, her feet on wood and glass.

Then at once she staggered to the door. Roger followed, choking on the fine down that had caught in his throat. Nancy was on the lawn, still hitting the air, and the rain fell in solid rods of water.

CHAPTER TWENTY-SIX

GWYN SCRAPED THE bowl for the last cornflake. Broken crackers were on the table. His mother had offered him nothing else, since he had been so late, and it was a relief when she interrupted her combined poking of the stove and nagging at him to eavesdrop on the argument upstairs.

He took a swig from the milk bottle.

The outer door of the kitchen banged, he heard a gasp, and then the inner door was pushed open and his mother fell into the kitchen. She swore and beat at an oilskin that shrouded her. The poker had ripped the fabric and was caught up in the folds, and both Nancy and the groundsheet were deep in feathers. Those that had been kept from the rain drifted about the kitchen, soaring in the heat of the stove.

Nancy struggled out of the oilskin and let it and the

poker drop to the floor. A wet piece of hair covered one eye and clung to her mouth. She scrubbed at it with a feathered hand.

"Get your mack," she said.

She went upstairs. Gwyn finished the milk, and watched the tawny feathers drift about the kitchen. He heard his mother in the flat, and the squeak of a strap, then two bumps. She moved on to the landing, and came down slowly, pulling a weight from step to step.

Gwyn sat at the table.

She had put on her mackintosh and a plastic rain hat which tied under the chin. "Come along," she said. "Carry them cases."

"Where we going?" said Gwyn.

"Aber."

"That's tomorrow."

"Shut your row, and do as you're told."

"How are we going?"

"Taxi to the station."

"That's twenty miles. How you getting a taxi?"

"Telephone. Move yourself, boy."

"Telephone's by the shop, and it's raining," said Gwyn.

"I'll not stay another minute," said Nancy. "Fetch your mack and them cases or you'll have a leathering, big as you are."

"Taxi's expensive," said Gwyn. "What's happened?"

"Never you mind."

"I'm not coming," said Gwyn. "You can look after your

own cases. I'm staying with my Dad."

Nancy had put on her gloves and was straightening the fingers when Gwyn spoke. She walked round the table, her hands frozen in the action.

"What's that, boy?"

"My Dad ran away," said Gwyn. "I shan't. I don't want to end up like him – or you."

Nancy brought her arm round and caught Gwyn at the side of the head. The blow knocked him off the chair. Nancy took his mackintosh from behind the door and threw it at him.

"Get up," she said. "Carry them cases."

"Why couldn't you ask properly the first time?" said Gwyn. "I'll carry the cases, but you'll see."

He dusted the feathers from his clothes, put on his mackintosh, lifted the two cases and went to the door. "It's raining," he said.

"Your cap's in your pocket."

"Shall I go and phone, and you wait with the cases?"

"No. I'm not staying here."

"Then you phone, and I'll wait."

"Shut your row, boy."

They set off along the drive. In the first yards the cold beat through to Gwyn's shoulders, then to his back, his legs, and then it was all over him and he was comfortable. He stuck out his tongue to catch the flow from his hair.

He had never seen rain spread visible in the sky, and its life was something he could feel as it dropped between him and the mountains. The mountains showed him rain a mile wide and a thousand feet high. He watched it all the way to the telephone box. Nancy hurried to walk and run at the same time, which made her knees buckle.

She was inside the box when Gwyn reached it, and she gestured to him to wait with the cases. He lodged them on a stone.

Waterfalls leapt at the skyline, where the day before there had been damp runnels. Gwyn thought of the Black Hiding.

Nancy was having trouble. She pressed button B.

People moved in the road. The shop bell rang. A woman walked behind a heifer. Bent men with sacks across their shoulders against the rain came out of hedge-banks and sheds. No one was in a hurry. Gwyn recognized a wall-eyed sheep dog, but it was not interested in him, though the people were. Before he realized it was happening there was a small crowd round the telephone box.

"Hello, boy."

"Is that your Mam phoning?"

"That Nancy, is it?"

"What she wanting that old phone for?"

"Where you going?"

"Suitcases, is it?"

"Nasty day."

"The wireless says flood warnings."

"You going anywhere, are you?"

"You going far?"

Some of it was in Welsh and some in English. He heard

the soft voices murmuring, not speaking to him, but a quiet conversation with him, among themselves.

Nancy pressed button A.

"We're leaving," said Gwyn. "Now. We're going to Aber. My Mam is phoning for a taxi to take us to the station. We're not coming back. We'll wait here for the taxi, and then we shan't ever come back. The taxi will be here in about half an hour."

"A taxi?"

"Where from, I wonder?"

"There's profligate."

"Always headstrong, your Mam."

"Had her own way, our Nancy."

"Taxis, now."

"Well, well."

The crowd thinned, dispersed, and the heifer went on up the road.

Nancy opened the door. "Taxi's coming," she said. "You wait there and mind them cases."

"I'll wait in the shop," said Gwyn.

"You won't. I'm not having you listen to no more talk. You stay there."

"It makes no odds."

"What was they on about just then?" said Nancy.

"You."

The door sighed, and shut her in. Gwyn practised filling the lace holes of his shoes with the water off his nose until the taxi came.

"Hurry up," said the driver. "Twenty minutes and we shan't get through for the river."

Gwyn put the cases in the boot while Nancy came out of the telephone box and scurried to the taxi.

"You coming as well, is it?" said the driver. "That's extra for wet seats."

"Get on," said Nancy.

The taxi started down the valley. When they passed the last cottage Nancy sank into the cushions.

The road was narrow, with hedges on either side, and it twisted up and down to find a way between the mountains and the river. The taxi had gone half a mile when the driver braked hard on a bend, throwing Nancy and Gwyn against the door.

"Careful, you fool!"

The taxi stopped. A tree had fallen across the road at the bottom of a hollow, and telephone wires coiled like springs along the ground. Two men stood at the other side of the hedge.

"Hello," one of them said.

"What the thump's going on here?" said the driver.

"She slipped when we were dropping her. Her roots — all the soil washed out by rain."

The driver went to Nancy. "What you want to do, Missis?"

"Clear the road," said Nancy.

"Don't be daft, Missis. Anyway, by the time this lot's right we'll be cut off by the river."

Chapter Twenty-Six

"Go the other side then, over the pass."

"Over the pass? That's dangerous in this weather: expensive."

"You go over that pass," said Nancy.

"Mind your heads," said the driver. "I can't see through the back window, and it's too narrow to turn here."

He reversed the taxi round the corner – and stopped. There was a tree across the road.

The driver climbed out, and shouted, but no one answered, and there was no one in sight.

"Well, Missis, that's it."

"That's it, Mam."

Nancy was wild-eyed. She held her handbag as if she thought it would be stolen, and she tugged at the door to open it.

"Where you going, Mam?"

She scrambled over the trunk and began to run back towards the house.

"What about money?" the taxi driver shouted. "This counts as waiting!"

"Bring the cases up the house when you're free," said Gwyn.

"You're don't see these cases till I see some money," said the driver. "I've had your sort before."

"That's right," said Gwyn. "Trust nobody."

He went after his mother. She had not run far. She was pushing herself on with her loose-kneed trot, and had reached the cottages. The rain was heavier, and the other side of the valley was behind cloud, but all along the road people were standing at their gates and in barn doorways, and Nancy had to pass them.

"Hello, Nancy."

"You been quick."

"Forgotten something, have you?"

"Changed your mind?"

"Aberystwyth too far, is it?"

"You go home, Nancy. You go home, pet."

"Not the weather to be out."

"Don't leave us, Nancy. Not twice, eh?"

"You go home, love."

"There's shocking weather."

"That's it, boy. You stay with your Mam."

"You look after her."

"Look after."

"Good boy."

"Good."

Gwyn followed Nancy, and said nothing, and she did not turn her head, but when she reached the front drive gate she hurried past it. Gwyn ran to catch up.

"You've missed the gate."

"I've not missed no gate." Her face was bone and thin as a man's.

"Where you going?"

"Where you think?"

"You can't walk the pass in this weather!"

The road went above the house and under the Bryn, and

the rain fell so that only hedges and trees could be seen and the fields were white. Gwyn's flesh throbbed with the water's bruising, and his mouth hung open.

"What am I supposed to do?"

"Do what you like, boy."

"Huw says I got to stay!"

"You stay, then."

"You don't care?" They were level with the back drive gate. "You don't care nothing? For me? For him? For this place? You never cared!"

"There isn't the pound notes in London—"

"I'm staying. Mam! I'm staying!"

Nancy receded from him, leaving him at the gate.

"Mam!"

She turned but did not stop. She walked backwards up the road, shouting, and the rain washed the air clean of her words and dissolved her haunted face, broke the dark line of her into webs that left no stain, and Gwyn watched for a while the unmarked place where she had been, then climbed over the gate.

CHAPTER TWENTY-SEVEN

ALISON SAT IN the window towelling her hair. She had heard a lot of movement in the house, and Roger had slammed in and out of his bedroom and was now running a bath.

The surface of the fish tank was like pewter under the rain. Nancy appeared on the drive and hurried away, and Gwyn followed more slowly with a case in each hand. He winced at the rain, and then turned his face up to catch the water in his mouth. The cases looked as though they were tugging his arms off. Each wrist came inches below the shirt cuff, and the mackintosh had rucked to the elbow. He followed Nancy along the drive, past the stables, out of sight.

Alison twisted the towel round her head and went downstairs to the first landing. The bath taps roared.

"Roger?"

"What?" He coughed and hawked.

"Is anything the matter?"

"It's disgusting."

"I think they've gone now," said Alison. "Nancy and Gwyn. Slipping off a day early when there's no one here. Mummy'll be livid. What shall we do?"

"I'm having a bath. These blasted feathers."

"Roger, shall I go after them?"

Roger was coughing too hard to answer.

Alison went to the cloakroom for her anorak and then out across the lawn, her hair still in its turban. The rain was like a wall.

They must have gone for a taxi. The phone box? Yes, they'd have to. I'll catch them there.

The road dropped between high banks. At the bottom was the bridge made of poor slate, and Alison saw a man grow out of the rain and stone as she came near. Huw Halfbacon leant on the bridge and watched the flood rise. He wore a sack pinned so that it hung down his back almost to the ground. The point of one corner reached his boots.

Alison hesitated. She pulled the turban out, and draped the towel across her arm, and shook her hair loose in the rain.

"Hello," said Huw. "Wet, isn't it?"

"Have you seen Nancy and Gwyn?" said Alison.

"They were going down the shop. They won't be long."

"Are you sure?" said Alison. "I think they're leaving."

"They will be back soon," said Huw. "They will not go."

"Why were they carrying their luggage?" said Alison.

"Practice, is it?" said Huw. "Now why are you getting so wet? You are not used to it like me. You will be catching chill. I am going back the house: come along now."

He turned Alison by her arm. "I got something for you," he said. "Present."

"A present? For me?" said Alison. "It's not my birthday."

"It is mean people who must wait for birthdays," said Huw. "No, no, this is just a present."

"What is it?" said Alison. "Are you sure they're coming back?"

"A present," said Huw. "I am certain of it."

They reached the back of the stables. Huw took out a key ring and fanned the keys. They were all worn smooth from his pocket.

"You never been in my part, have you?"

"No," said Alison. "Look, that door's open."

"Yes, she's loose now," said Huw.

"I must tell Roger. What's in it?"

"Nothing," said Huw. He unlocked his own low green door and steered Alison inside. "You will excuse the untidy."

It was a room of bare stone and a sloping roof with massive cross beams, and at first there was no suggestion that it was lived in. It was a lumber room in an outhouse, cluttered with boxes and crates, paint cans, oil drums, ropes, mallets, rusted tools, and tins of nails, a chimney sweep's brush and rods. There was no furniture, but planks side by side bridged two beams, and on them Alison saw blankets, and a sack of straw for a pillow.

"You – live – here?" she said.

"Yes," said Huw. "Always."

"How long?"

"Always. I am not good at counting years."

"But there's nowhere to sit, or to cook, no water, no fire. How do you manage? What happens in winter?"

"Winter is a cold time, yes," said Huw.

"Where do you keep things?" said Alison. "Clothes."

"I wear clothes," said Huw. "And I got all the valley to keep things in. But special things: here."

He rummaged in the blankets.

"Present for you," he said.

"I don't want it," said Alison. "That's a beastly trick."

Huw held out the box. "It is yours," he said. "The present is inside."

"I know what's inside. I don't want it." She pressed herself against a metal bunker. "Don't bring it near me."

Huw opened the box. "It is special present from the boy. He asked special. All I done is put that old lace on."

"What?" Alison looked down at the box which Huw held in front of her. The polished slate glowed, and the shape of brow and eye stood clear in the dim light. A leather bootlace was threaded through the hole so that the pendant could be worn.

"He is saying it is very old." Huw took the pendant out of the box.

"It's too awful — I can't bear it."

"It is yours. The boy said to give it you for present."

"No."

"He wants you to have it, but he is shy to give himself."

"Put it away! Please! It's too much!"

"No, no, very cheap, nothing at all. I am saying you give it her, boy, but no you give her he is saying, and tell her it is from me. He is a nice boy."

"No! — Please not!"

Huw lifted the pendant and slipped the bootlace over her head.

"There. Present for you."

Roger put on clean clothes. The barbs of feather had lodged everywhere, and the dust and smell were still foul in his throat. He opened the bedroom window to clear the air — and he saw Huw Halfbacon come from the back of the stables. The rain moved behind him, the earth boiled as if under a harrow, and he was carrying Alison over his shoulder.

"What's wrong?" Roger called.

"She fainted there. It was present from the boy, then wallop on the bunker."

"Is she hurt?"

"Let us in quick, and fetch the boy."

Roger ran to the kitchen.

"Bar the door," said Huw. He laid Alison on the table.

"What's up with her?" said Roger. "Who's scratched her face?"

Alison's cheek was scored with parallel red lines, but they seemed to be under the skin. There was no bleeding.

"Go fetch the boy," said Huw. "Tell him be quick."

"She wants a doctor," said Roger.

"Go fetch that boy!" shouted Huw. He marched Roger to the door and threw him outside.

"It's wet, you crackpot! Let me in! I've just changed!" Huw had bolted the door. Roger hurried to the cloakroom, was too late, and the front door was locked.

He ran all the way down the drive and the road to the telephone box. The line was dead: silence in his ear. He went into the shop.

"Yes?" said Mrs Richards.

"Telephone," said Roger.

"Wires are down," said Mrs Richards. "Tree fallen on the road. Shocking weather, isn't it? They say it's worse along the valley."

"How can I find a doctor?"

"You can't find no doctor. What you want a doctor for?"

"It's Miss Alison. She's fainted: or concussed. I don't know."

"You find Gwyn," said Mrs Richards. "You'll be all right. The poor girl. You go find him now. He's up the house."

Roger backed out of the shop.

"Gwyn! Gwyn! Gwyn!"

He searched the garden as far as the wood. He fought through nettles and swamp to the drive, and when he reached the level ground he could hardly stand. Gwyn was climbing over the gate from the road.

"Gwyn!"

Gwyn sat on the gate.

"Gwyn! Halfbacon wants you! He says be quick! The kitchen! – Wait for me!"

But Gwyn went without speaking to Roger. Below him the wood held a noise that came closer, yet was hard to place among the trees, and the rain and the river crashed in flood, and the one noise itself was the total of all its sounds. If it was anything it was the noise of a wind on the pass and its echo before it in the valley, or it was the noise of owls hunting, though he had never heard so many: never a wood of owls.

"Huw! Huw, man! Huw! Huw!" Roger caught up with Gwyn while Huw was unfastening the bolts. "What is it, Huw? What's happened?"

"Come in, boy."

Alison lay on the table, covered with Huw's jacket. Feathers clung to her and drifted round her. Huw brushed them off, and they circled with the convection currents, and came back to her.

"It's the power," said Huw. "It's in her now, bad. This is it, boy."

"'What do you want me to do?" said Gwyn.

"Help her."

"Her there? Or her outside?"

"They are the same now," said Huw.

The wind hit the house. Blossom and twigs flew by,

stripped from the bushes, the tendrils of clematis cracked on the walls and leaves stuck to the window and skylight in a green autumn. Rain washed them off, gravel let pinholes of day through. More leaves came.

"I've stayed to help you and the valley, not this lot," said Gwyn. "These two are nothing."

"You are the three. You have made this together," said Huw.

"I'm not doing anything for them. I've finished."

Roger brushed the feathers away from Alison. They circled and clung: circled and clung: the owl dance he had found in the dust. They were moving on the ceiling and the walls, and he began to see the patterns that had followed Huw in the rain: eyes and wings and sharpness: winged eyes, yellow, and blackness curved: all in the rafters and the wall and the feathers everywhere. There had never been so many feathers. He brushed them from Alison's cheek. She cried out, and he saw three lines scored from brow to neck, and on her hands, and no break in the skin.

"Stop jabbering, you, and do something," said Roger. "Get these feathers off. Get them off!"

"I am not knowing what to do," said Huw.

"You said you did know," said Gwyn. "What's gone wrong?"

"You."

"Why me? I'm here. I've not run away. You said this was my valley, and I've not run away. I promised not to. I trusted you last night, and came back. Show me what I've to do."

"I can't – say."

"What?" said Gwyn.

"I only feel. Always it is owls, always we are destroyed. Why must she see owls and not flowers? Always it is the same."

"What is it you want me to do?" said Gwyn.

"Look to her. Comfort her."

"I can't."

"Just comfort her."

"I can't, man. Anything else. You don't know what these two have done. I can't touch her."

Alison trembled. Claw marks dragged at her legs.

"She is coming, and will use what she finds, and you have only hate in you," said Huw. "Always and always and always."

Gwyn's jaw was fixed.

"Try," said Huw.

"You didn't say it would be this," said Gwyn. "I can't."

"Try. Comfort."

"No."

"Comfort."

Gwyn shook his head.

The skylight smashed under a branch, but the wires bonded in the glass kept out the weight that pressed to enter, and in the darkness the feathers and the eyes and the claws hung and moved. The kitchen was swept with rain. There was no colour in Alison's face except for the scratches. Her breath came quick and shallow.

"Can't you stop it?" said Roger.

"He can," said Huw. "But he is not wanting."

"Can't you make him? Why not?"

"He was hurt too much. He is not telling me."

"You won't do this," Roger said to Gwyn. "It's Ali."

Gwyn did not move.

Roger put out his hand, but Gwyn ignored him. "Gwyn." Roger spoke quietly. "It's my fault. It was me. Not Ali. She never laughed at you. It wasn't like I said. I twisted it round. I'm sorry. Don't let it happen, Gwyn. If you really can stop it, don't let it happen."

Gwyn turned his head and looked at Roger. Roger saw the question form in his eyes, and he saw that Gwyn knew.

"All right, Gwyn?"

The blue of the eyes froze, and in a slow voice Gwyn said, "Get lost – Mummy's boy."

The walls were shedding their texture and taking another in the pouncing feathers. Gwyn spoke again, but Roger could scarcely hear across the darkness. "Yes. Yes, Gwyn." The back of his head and all his spine were hollow. There was bile in his throat. He could do nothing to answer the words. He could only shore his mind against them, because if he did not he would be spilled by the bitter dark.

"And how is the Birmingham Belle? Still ringing?

"Yes, Gwyn."

There was no more.

He waited, but there was no more, and in the calm of the pain's clearing he found no anger. Gwyn stood alone. Huw crouched by the stove. Roger looked at them both, the man and the boy. "You poor devils," he said.

He went to Alison and gathered the feathers that lay on her.

"You poor devils."

"He is hurt too much she wants to be flowers and you make her owls and she is at the hunting—"

"Is that it?" said Roger. "Is that all it is? As easy as that?"

"—and so without end without end without end—"

"Hey, Ali, did you hear?" Roger brushed the feathers aside. "You've got it back to front, you silly gubbins. She's not owls. She's flowers. Flowers. Flowers, Ali." He stroked her forehead. "You're not birds. You're flowers. You've never been anything else. Not owls. Flowers. That's it. Don't fret."

Alison stirred.

"Oh yes they are flowers! And you know it! Flowers, Ali. Quietly, now. Flowers. Flowers. Flowers. Gentle. Flowers—"

He pulled Huw's jacket higher, and turned the collar to keep off the rain. Alison tugged it down between her shoulder and chin. Roger laughed.

"Flowers. Flowers. That's the way." The marks paled on her skin, and tightness went from her face as she breathed to the measure of his hand on her brow. "That's better. There now: yes: yes: of course they're flowers. What made you think those plates could be anything else? Why didn't you cut the pattern into flowers right at the start, you silly girl?"

"By damn," said Huw.

Chapter Twenty-Seven

Something touched Roger's hand. He started to brush it away, but there were too many. He looked up.

"Hello, Ali."

And the room was full of petals from skylight and rafters, and all about them a fragrance, and petals, flowers falling, broom, meadowsweet, falling, flowers of the oak.

Postscript

The Owl Service is a kind of ghost story, in real life as well as on the page. Right from the start things happened that had not happened with earlier books.

It began when I read an old Welsh legend about Lleu, and his wife Blodeuwedd who was made for him out of flowers. Later she fell in love with Gronw Pebr, and together they murdered Lleu. Lleu was brought back to life by magic, and he killed Gronw by throwing a spear with such force that it went right through the rock behind which Gronw was sheltering; and the rock, says the legend, is called The Stone of Gronw to this day. Blodeuwedd, for her part in her husband's murder, was turned into an owl.

When I read the legend, I felt that it was not just a magical tale, but a tragedy of three people who destroy each other through no fault of their own but just because they were forced together. It was a modern story: the idea that you could have three people for some reason unable to get away from each other, and I began to think about how I could bring them into that position, and what sort of people would they have to be to interact so lethally and yet be harmless in themselves.

The legend stuck in my mind for several years, and then one day my mother-in-law showed me an old dinner service. She had noticed that the floral pattern round the edge of the plates could be seen as the body, wings and head of an owl. My wife, Griselda, traced the pattern, juggled it a bit, folded the pattern together and there it was, a model paper owl, which she perched on the back of a chair.

An owl from flowers. A woman made from flowers and changed into an owl. I saw at once that here, in this dinner service, was my modern story, based on the legend. But even so, for a long time nothing else would come. Then, by chance, we went to stay at a house in a remote valley in North Wales. Within hours of arriving I knew that I had found the setting for the story, or the setting had found me. Its atmosphere fitted both the original legend and the nature of the dinner service. Ideas began to grow. Suppose three people came here to this house and found the plates. Suppose the plates held the power of the legend, like batteries. The story took shape. I looked around for more ideas. The lie of the land fitted the descriptions in the legend. Everything was where it ought to be. The legend could have happened here. As I stood on the doorstep at night, thinking these things, an owl brushed its wings in my face.

The sensation of finding, not inventing, a story continued. It was all there, waiting, and I was the archaeologist picking away the earth to reveal the bones.

Dafydd Rees was eighty-one years old. He was known in the valley as Clocydd, "bell-ringer", because he had rung the church bell for sixty-five years, after his uncle retired from the same job after seventy years. Dafydd had worked as the caretaker and gardener of the house since 1898. He was the greatest help to me, since he let me in to his knowledge of the valley, its history, its traditions, its folklore. Everything that Gwyn, in the book, tells Alison about the valley, is what Dafydd told me. But although he knew that I was writing a story about the valley, I never mentioned the legend to him, nor he to me. So it was a shock one day when I was walking in the rain and came upon Dafydd sitting in the hedgebank, a sack about his shoulders, and scratching a flat piece of slate with a pointed one. I sat down to talk, and looked at what he was doing. He had scratched the world "Blodeuwedd" on the flat slate.

"What's that?" I said.

"A name," said Dafydd.

"Can you tell me about it?"

"It's just a name," said Dafydd, and threw the slate into the river.

"Has anyone ever been killed here?" I said.

"Yes," said Dafydd.

"How?"

"Bow and arrow. A Red Indian stood on the hill just by there, and shot the man at a stone near the river. Perhaps he escaped from Buffalo Bill's circus that was at Dolgellau that time, the Indian. Funny old tale, isn't it?"

But Dafydd told me nothing of Lleu, Blodeuwedd and Gronw Pebr; and I knew better than to ask.

The Owl Service was made into a television series, for which I wrote the script, and we filmed it in the valley. I found the experience hard to bear, because characters – who had lived in my head for so many years – were now really in the valley and really speaking the words that I had written. What had been a thought was now happening in front of me. It felt like a kind of magical madness. But, after nine weeks, it was over, and all the concentration that had made the story and the actors more real than reality ended instantly, with the director's command of "Cut!"

The cameras stopped, the lights went out, the gear was stowed, the costumes were packed, the actors cleaned off their make-up and went their ways, to become once more individuals, never again to be together in that relationship. They went.

For me, in the valley where I had set the story, it was a sense of loss. The valley had not changed. It was as it had been before I ever knew it. For a few hectic weeks my thoughts had taken on shapes, and moved as people in the landscape where I had imagined them. But now they had gone, and all was as it had always been.

"It was a good time," Dafydd wrote in a letter afterwards. "I have been to the stone. She is lonely now."

ALAN GARNER